S0-AZP-655

The Face in My Window

Margo Huver and Janet Dick

© 2017 Margo Huver and Janet Dick
All rights reserved.

ISBN: 0692812946
ISBN 13: 9780692812945
Library of Congress Control Number: 2016960845
Peony Press, Grand Rapids, Michigan

I have lived a very interesting life.
Several times I have wondered, *Why?*
What do these experiences have to do with me?
Why did this happen to me?
Sometimes we find out.
Most times, we don't.

Thank you to family and friends who encouraged the completion of this book.

Prologue

What I have always known that I needed to do, that I was compelled to do, that I should have done a long, long, time ago... was write my story. But I feared for the safety of my family, especially my small children. The face in my window traumatized me. Who was this man behind those dark vacant eyes?

At the time of the stalking, I tried to get the police involved to no avail. Thankfully, my family and neighbors did all they could to support and protect me.

The frightening happenings of 1966 and 1968 were always in the back of my mind. Still, my life was very rich and full. My husband, Duane Francis (he was always called Butch), with help from me built a strong business. We met the demands and reaped the rewards of raising our children and guiding them toward successful careers.

We grieved over the loss of our parents. We more than delighted in grandbabies.

1969 was the beginning of a new family tradition...camping. That summer was when I told my story for the first time around a campfire in Pentwater, Michigan, on the shores of Lake Michigan. Though I was asked many times to tell my story, it was just that....My Story. Unlike other campfire tales, this was very real to me. It shook me to the core every time I told it!

When we first started camping we would crowd into a little pop-up camper, but we later graduated to a motor home. By this time, seven other families and their extended families had joined us. One of the children would always come get me and drag me to the campfire so I could tell my stories. I began with their favorite one by staring into the fire and following the red-gold sparks and the gray smoke up into the night air. Then looking around at all their expectant faces, I would tell my story. As the years went by, their children and their children's children heard the same tale.

Now, more than four decades later, I'm no longer afraid to reveal my story. I can't help but think that if the forensics of today had been available in the sixties, and women were taken more seriously, history just might have been changed.

Part I

Chapter One

The 1960s

Butch and I had been married for six years. We were twenty-five years old and had four children under five. Blond with blue-gray eyes and five feet eight inches tall, my husband was a James Dean look-alike, especially in his blue jeans and white T-shirt and the occasional pack of cigarettes tucked in his rolled-up sleeve. I loved the twinkle in his eye and his subtle swagger. Our five-year-old, Seamus, was tall and solid for his age. He had blond curls and almost lapis-blue eyes, and he was the definition of the word "mischievous." Todd, almost four and very feisty, was blond with deep brown eyes. Anne, at two, a true towhead with round, brown eyes, was our well-behaved and sweet princess. Our chubby baby, Danny, at nine months old, had inherited my dark hair and Butch's blue eyes. He crawled all over and was trying very hard to stand.

We lived in Grand Rapids, Michigan, with its population around 160,000. It was noted as a true family community. The downtown was divided by the wide Grand River and was only about three-square miles. Although small, the central area was sophisticated, a mini metropolis with stately buildings of both distinguished vintage and modern architecture. The tallest structure at the time was McKay Tower, almost considered a skyscraper. High-end restaurants as well as popular greasy spoons such as the Knife and Fork were within the downtown boundaries.

Everyone shopped at Herpolsheimer's Department Store, the desired destination for the latest fashion and home-furnishing trends. The wonderful tea room was a destination for bridge ladies, families, and business luncheons. The store's nickname was the Great Divide because half was dedicated to Michigan State University, complete with green carpeting, the school's colors, and the other half was dedicated to the University of Michigan, with blue-and-gold carpeting. At Christmas time, a decorated train, the Santa Express, followed a track along the ceiling, delighting all the children and those who came to Herps during the holidays. Every season, the vast expanse of the windows from Monroe to Division Street was filled with moving displays according to the holidays.

Since the early nineteenth century, Grand Rapids had been the furniture capital of the Midwest. As early as 1878, one company boasted 450 different styles of chairs. Several colleges existed in the area, the latest being White Rapids College, WRC, established in 1960. The neighborhoods surrounding the business district consisted of mostly wooden frame homes on narrow streets. The larger red-brick homes sat back on deeper lots along wide, curving, oak and elm tree-lined streets. No matter the neighborhood, residents were just minutes from downtown. Small rural towns and rich flat farmland surrounded all of Grand Rapids.

Our cozy neighborhood consisted of modest two-story white frame homes built in the 1930s, standing very close together on small lots with just room for a driveway between. There were no fences between the yards or at the backs of the homes. The backyards sloped down a hill to a small open industrial area. On the front porches, two pillars supported a pointed overhang. Those porches often saw children playing Monopoly or rummy, mothers chatting and smoking Tareytons, and fathers slugging down Pabst Blue Ribbon or Stroh's beer. Scraggly trees grew here and there near the curb along our street.

The neighborhood was mixed with elderly who had lived there for a very long time and midlife couples with teenagers; we were one of the young ones, just starting out. The men were pretty much employed as accountants, factory workers, train engineers, bartenders, or pressmen. Most of the women tended the children and took care of the home. Everyone shopped for groceries at the new superstore, Meijer. Around the corner from our house was the typical Michigan party store, offering beer, alcohol, mixers, chips, pretzels, and nuts, as well as bread and milk.

In winter, Radio Flyer sleds were pulled on the seldom-plowed, snowy streets, and lopsided snowmen stood guard in front of several homes. In the summer, the postage-stamp lawns had little boys playing cowboys and Indians, running from yard to yard, and little girls playing dress-up or movie stars or Barbies and wanting our babies to join in. Anne and Danny were the entertainment of the neighborhood, since they were the only babies there. The older children took turns pushing them in the stroller or cajoling them to play "house." I spent a lot of time on the front stoop watching all these scenarios unfold.

When our youngest was six weeks old, Butch excitedly sat me down at the kitchen table and took both my hands.

"Honey," he said, "what don't I like about working at GM? What do I complain about?"

"Butch! You didn't lose your job, did you? My God...our house, the kids..."

"No. No. Just answer my question."

"Um...you don't like how a lot of the guys dog it and don't work as hard as they could and are really costing the company profits? Um...you say you know everything about precision grinding and are the best at it?"

"Right! So I talked to your dad..."

"My dad? What the—"

"Just listen, Margo. Just listen. He agreed to help us get a five-hundred-dollar loan so I can open up my own shop... our own shop. He's all for it. He said he has confidence in me. Gotta love that guy."

"But what are we going to live on? Will you do this all by yourself? I just don't know. This is crazy."

"Of course, I will stay at GM and work on this part time. I know I can do it. And you can help out with the books and stuff. You're smart and can learn how. Really, honey, this is a great opportunity for us."

I had not seen him so excited since our first baby was born. His eyes were like firecrackers, and he had begun pacing around the kitchen. He had said my dad was OK with this. And then the man I loved was almost on his knees, pleading. I said, "All right. All right. But you'll be so tired. What about the kids?"

Butch put both hands on the table and leaned his face close to mine.

"I know. Your dad said that this was asking a lot from you. But I promise, this whole deal will be worth it."

A whirlwind of questions, objections, and possibilities whipped around in my head. But his enthusiasm sucked me in.

"Sure. Let's do it."

Butch let out a whoop and jumped around the room. He reminded me of my little brothers when my uncle had given them tickets for box seats at a Tigers game. I was not ready to jump around, but I was ready to give this man a huge hug, and, as the song went, "seal it with a kiss."

My father cosigned a five-hundred-dollar loan for the leasing of two precision grinding machines and the renting of a small factory space we called "the shop." Butch worked there days from eight a.m. to two p.m., came home for the dinner I prepared, changed his clothes, and then went off to the afternoon shift from three p.m. to midnight at General Motors. The man never complained. He seemed to be positively energized by the building of his new business. I existed like a widow, but I had a living husband. Once, when our car was spilling over with grungy little boys after playing at the park, a friend of my son's said, "I think there really *is* a Mr. Huver!" This was a difficult time for us, and it was compounded by our baby's health issue.

Little Danny had been very ill with breathing difficulties since he was six weeks old and was on various antibiotics, none of which seemed to work. Many nights, I would sit at the bottom of the stairs, listening to him struggle for breath. I would find myself attempting to breathe for him and praying for him to get better.

On Christmas Day at my parents' home, Danny's face turned very red, and he became listless, a little lump in my arms. My mother took charge.

"This isn't right. This is serious. I'm calling my doctor."

Danny was admitted to the hospital immediately. After ten days, we were sent to an allergist and found out that this little baby was allergic to a myriad of things, including milk and our German shepherd, Chip. We traveled to a farm every other day for fresh goat's milk, and Dan's room had to be emptied of everything. Each day the crib, floor, window, and windowsills had to be washed and rinsed and fresh cheesecloth put over the registers. Each night I had to vacuum Chip's fur and keep him from coming up past the landing. I was exhausted. There were nights when I thought I heard noises at the side door, but I was too tired to go look.

Chapter Two

The First Encounter

This particular night in January 1966 was cold, with half a foot of snow on the ground. A full moon illuminated our neighborhood. Around eleven thirty, Butch called from the payphone outside the restrooms at the General Motors plant.

"Margo, I really need to go back out to the shop tonight. A job came in that needs to be completed by early morning. I know you were looking forward to me being home for the evening, but I just can't. Honey, would you please make me a couple sandwiches and a pot of coffee?"

"OK. See you soon."

This was nothing new. My worrying about him working so many hours and losing precious sleep had become commonplace.

I sighed and then put together two of his favorite ham, salami, and Miracle Whip sandwiches, brewed a fresh pot of coffee, and added a Hostess cupcake. I knew he would love this treat. Around twelve fifteen in the morning, he arrived home and gratefully picked up his lunch and thermos. He decided to take our dog, Chip, with him for company. This was a good idea because our little factory space was at the back of a huge, empty warehouse. At night it was a bit spooky. Little did

I know that "spooky" would not even come close to describing the coming events of that night.

Butch hugged me and kissed the top of my head. "You're the best." I watched out the front door as he threw the lunch on the front seat of our white van and hustled the dog into the back.

After he pulled away, I made myself half of a ham sandwich, cleaned up the counter, and took the sandwich and a bottle of Pepsi into our den. We had converted the small formal dining room into a den and playroom. Fancy dinner parties were not part of our young, struggling lives at that time, and during the day, many hours were spent playing on the floor with the children. The day's toys filled four red crates in the corner. That night, I did not bother to turn on the light, as I planned to watch the rest of Johnny Carson while I ate, check on each sleeping little one, and then head off to bed.

The den had four windows, two on the front of the house and two on the driveway side. I had covered them with white cotton cafe curtains with a ruffled trim. Soon I was getting a little chilly. The variegated green rug I was crocheting for our living room was spread across the other end of the couch. I leaned over to pull it onto my legs and noticed that the crack between the curtains on one window on the driveway side was light like the rest of the windows, but when I straightened up, the crack was dark. Because of the full moon, the streetlight and the large white house on the other side of our driveway, it was easy to see into the night. Why was that one window dark?

I was alone in a two-story house with my four babies, who were all asleep upstairs. I thought, *Margo, you need to look and make sure nothing is out there. You know you won't be able to sleep if you don't check it out*. I jumped up, the rug went flying, and the crochet hook clattered on the hardwood floor (that *ding, ding, ding* still echoes in my memory). I pulled the curtains apart, and I saw a thick, black head of hair scrunched flat against the window. I was not yet afraid, musing that one of my fun-loving cousins would think it hilarious to try to scare me. They had pulled numerous pranks at my expense in the past.

I rapped my knuckles against the window, but the face that looked up was not that of a cousin. Besides the thick, black hair, this man had a large nose, black, beady eyes with a weirdly vacant stare, and an olive complexion. The clear image of him would be fixed in my mind forever—and I mean forever. He wore a neatly pressed, white dress shirt and a dark-blue or black windbreaker...odd for such a cold winter night. Terrified, I pounded and pounded on the window, screaming at the same time, but he would not move. He just continued to stare at me, not ten inches from my face. "Oh my God! Help me!" I screamed so loudly and hysterically that my throat was hot and scratched. Eventually, my voice gave out.

Finally, he turned and casually walked down the driveway toward the street. I darted to the front window so I could tell the police which direction he went. When I parted the curtain just a fraction, he was only about ten feet away. He couldn't possibly have heard the light cotton material moving. At that same second, he turned around and looked me right in the eyes with his vacant, frightening stare. As he walked away, his pace did not quicken at all. I knew I could also identify him by his rear end. It was not flat, but one that filled out his dark, pressed pants.

Shaking all over, I fell to the floor and reached for the phone on the round mahogany table between the windows. The lacy white doily from my grandmother slipped to the floor as I grabbed the phone, I tried to steady my hands as I dialed information for the number and called the police.

I knew Butch had a deadline to finish this job. He was working so hard at both places, striving to be successful, so I didn't want to bother or scare him. There was nothing he could do anyway; the police were on their way. But I didn't want to be alone.

My next phone call woke my neighbor, Chris. Her husband, Andy, had a chronic heart condition but could sleep through anything. Chris was over in minutes. Her gray herringbone coat was thrown over a pale-yellow robe, and pink bristly rollers lined her whole head in perfect rows. Now I was shaking not only from fear but from being so cold. It was like a switch had been turned on internally, changing my warm blood into icy trickles. Chris grabbed my navy pea coat from the front closet and draped it over me. We sat huddled, shoulder to shoulder, on the couch.

Impatient, I soon stood up and peeked out the side curtains to look for the police. I shuddered at the grease stain on my window from that black hair. "That's got to come off! That's got to come off!" I shrieked.

"Tomorrow, Margo. Tomorrow, Margo," Chris replied. She stood up and hugged me, guiding me back to the couch.

Finally, a police car slowly crackled across the snow-packed street and parked at our front curb, its circling light like a red sprinkler on the white lawn. I ran to open the door, and a baby-faced policeman stood on the porch. He did not come in. "Ma'am, I understand you thought you saw a prowler?"

"I don't *think* I saw someone. I *did* see someone...right there at the side window. His hair was dark and thick and greasy, and he—"

"Ma'am," the officer interrupted, "it's past midnight. It's dark. How can you be sure what he looked like?"

"Because we were face-to-face for several seconds, maybe even twenty! I know what I saw. And he had on a white shirt, real crisp...and a navy-blue windbreaker. And he had a full butt."

"What? A full butt?" He straightened up and tilted his head back. "Lady, what do you mean?"

"I mean a full butt. Not a flat one. His pants were filled out. I noticed this when he walked away, right down my driveway—right there!"

"OK, OK. I'll file the report. And we'll be on the lookout for this guy."

I stared up at him. "Aren't you going to walk around the house and check out the area, look for footprints—something?"

"Look. We get calls like this all the time from women. I'm sure you scared him more than he scared you."

"But...but...the guy stayed in the window, right in my face. And he didn't run away. He just walked away, and..."

"Ma'am. We have all the information we need. Now, just relax, and you have a good night." He turned, hunched his shoulders against the cold, and carefully walked down the slippery porch steps, leaving me standing at our door, stunned.

What I had just experienced was the most frightening event of my entire life. My body was still shaking both inside and out, and my voice was barely audible. And the policeman, the type of person I had always looked up to—and for protection—had been demeaning and dismissive. What a letdown. If he didn't believe me, who would? What if I needed the police in the future?

But Chris was still there.She was about ten years older than me, cute with sparkly green eyes and deep dimples when she smiled. She was the happy neighborhood nurse, the one to take shopping when I needed a special dress, the best pal to share a pot of coffee with or maybe even a highball. She had now become Chris, a reliable friend and ally.

We remained on the couch, trying to chat about anything inconsequential. But I always returned to saying, "That face, that face...that weird, blank stare. What was he doing here? Why didn't he move?"

The Grand Rapids Police Department building, established in the late 1800s, stood at the corner of Crescent and Ottawa and had been designed after the style of a talented but not often recognized architect named H. H. Richardson. The headquarters sported large, rectangular, dark-brown, horizontal stones. The fourth floor had pointed roof lines and tall arched windows. Rectangular windows surrounded the third floor, and the second-floor arched windows were smaller with faded blue-and-white-striped awnings on the sunny side of the building. The first floor, with small barred windows, housed the jail. (Over the years, many had remarked that it should take only one stay in that old dank dungeon to deter a person from any further crimes. Alas, it was not so true.) The abandoned Fox de Luxe Brewery building just north of the police department housed the police cruisers.

Robby Ellison, age twenty-one, parked his cruiser at the brewery and strode across the small adjacent parking lot, in through the main doors, and up a flight of worn, gray marble stairs to the general office. Sergeant Al Grubowski, sixty-three, sat behind a large, scarred oak desk. His sleeves were rolled up, exposing a lot of white hair covering his thick forearms. He was just finishing a sub sandwich, wiping his mouth with a coarse paper napkin. Smaller desks were scattered around the room, a few with officers leaning over paperwork. "So. How did it go, rookie? Let me guess. GOA."

"Yep, Sarge. Gone on arrival."

"Always are. And what was the lady like? A looker?"

"Actually, yes. A *That Girl* type."

"What girl?"

"You know, the TV show with Marlo Thomas? *That Girl*? This gal had the same long, dark hair that flips up. Nice figure, pretty."

"Oh, yeah. I don't watch it; the wife does. So, what was the babe's story?"

"Said a guy was looking in her window and didn't move when she opened the curtains. Had a funny look. She was pretty scared. A neighbor gal was with her. Husband was at work. Couldn't do much to calm her down. Took the info and left. Man, it's freezing out tonight."

"OK, Robby. Got your cruiser card filled out?"

"Yep. Gonna put it in the file. See ya, Sarge."

Robby fished the three-by-five card out of his pocket and tossed it into the box on top of a green metal file cabinet.

Sergeant Grubowski mused, as he watched Robby practically skip down the stairs, *I remember having all that energy at the end of a shift and meeting the guys for a couple of beers and bullshitting. Not anymore. That's for sure*, he mused.

He looked forward to crawling into his warm bed and cuddling next to his wife.

In the parking lot, Robby smiled, realizing how much he loved sliding into his canary-yellow 1965 Mustang. The car had been a gift for graduating from the academy the previous year. His Uncle Harry owned a large furniture-manufacturing plant, and he had never had children. He loved sharing his wealth with his niece and nephew.

Everyone should have a rich Uncle Harry, he thought. I'm so lucky to have no car payments and to be living with my parents for a while. I can save money for my future…maybe a cute wife like that Mrs. Huver, a house, and some kids. I better be making more than my forty-one hundred a year by then. He also hoped more exciting stuff would be happening on his beat besides phantom prowlers.

Butch came home around three thirty in the morning."What's going on? Oh my God! Chris, what are you doing here? Are the kids OK? Margo…what the hell?"

I choked out my story, this time between gasps and sobs. Chris filled in the blanks. Then Butch helped her on with her coat and walked her to the door.

"Thanks. Thanks so much, Chris…for being here for Margo, in the middle of the night, no less."

"Anytime," Chris said. "No, wait a minute. No more times like this! That's for sure. Get to bed, you two." We watched her pad across the street and into her home.

Butch held me and smoothed my hair. "I am so sorry you had to go through this. I really wish I had been home."

"And that policeman…" I almost spit out the words.

"Honey, I really don't think this will happen again. Our locks are strong, and we have the dog. And you better believe I will always leave him home with you from now on. Let's get to bed."

Somewhat reassured and suddenly very tired, I turned to go up the stairs with him to try for at least a few hours' sleep. But first, I checked on Seamus, who was on his back with the covers scrunched between his legs. Todd, on his side, was lying horizontally across the top of his bed. Clutching her blue calico baby doll was Anne, with her face smashed into her pillow. Baby Danny was in my favorite baby position...on his tummy, knees under his chest, his Carter's-clad little rear-end sticking up, and his thumb in his mouth. All were innocently asleep. As I did each night, I covered them all and blew them kisses.

Around one in the morning, Rosemary Vander, a neighbor, gave the hammered copper bar a final wipe before closing up. The Red Rocket Lounge sat on the outskirts of town, close to the freeway that traveled straight up the Lower Peninsula all the way to the Mackinac Bridge, which connected to Michigan's pristine Upper Peninsula. The tavern's walls were authentic knotty pine, complemented by mud-green and faded gold-speckled linoleum floors, cracked red Naugahyde barstools, and worn pine tables and chairs. The clientele consisted of regulars and tourists from Chicago or southwest Michigan on their way up north. The Red Rocket offered one-third-pound hamburgers with or without American cheese, real French fries cooked in beef tallow, and cold Stroh's beer.

Rosemary tossed the dishrag into the tub to be washed later and hung her red-and-white checkered apron adorned with a red rocket on the front onto a hook in the storeroom. After checking that the tavern was respectable, she turned off the lights, locked the door, bundled up, and walked to her car.

At close one fifteen a.m., she slowly drove up her driveway and past her house, idling the car in front of the garage for a moment. Once out of the car, she walked gingerly on the snow-packed cement up to the garage door, which seemed especially heavy tonight after she had worked the late shift. Back in the car, she inched into the garage and thought she saw a flash of someone or something through the narrow horizontal window on the back wall of her garage. Her pulse quickened as she got out of the car, but her husband, Phil, was waiting for her, holding their side door open. Rosemary shrugged and figured that she probably hadn't really seen anything. She hurried into the house.

Another neighbor, eighty-one-year-old Shirley Cracco couldn't sleep, so she warmed some milk, poured it into her favorite blue Wedgewood cup, and stirred in a teaspoon of honey. She stood by her front window, holding the soothing cup with both hands and peering out into the deserted street. Surprised, she saw that lady, Chris, hustle across the street. It looked to Shirley as if she had come from the house of that young woman down the street with all the little kids. As Shirley sat down on her plastic-covered sofa, sipping her milk, she considered whom she could ask about it tomorrow.

The next morning, my story flew around the neighborhood. I later heard that the nosy old lady down the street had clucked that the prowler had probably seen me in my bathing suit in the backyard during the summer and wanted another look. So this was my fault? What a biddy!

That afternoon, the phone rang. It was Rosemary from a few houses down. She told me she heard the buzz about my frightening encounter.

"There was someone out there, Margo. I think it was your prowler hiding behind my garage watching your house, saw the police, and Chris coming over. It was around one fifteen a.m., probably just after the incident at your house." She took a breath. "I checked behind my garage this morning and found footprints and five or six cigarette butts lying on top of the snow."

Chapter Three

A Rallying and a Stakeout

Ice-blue Windex squirted on the frosty window; paper towel attacked that grease stain. I had to obliterate it.

The sun was shining; the air was frigid. The sky was a brilliant blue, and the children were happy. Yet all I could think of was what I was going to do when darkness came. I was really, really afraid. Why had this man been at my window? Why did he stare at me for so long and not run away? And that odd, vacant look? Would he be back? Was it him rattling the back doorknob those other late nights? No one could know what I was experiencing. I felt violated and was terrified. The police officer's flippant remark had shattered my confidence and left me very insecure. I knew what I'd seen; why didn't that man believe me? I was floating without a safety net.

But soon, standing at the now-clean window with my shoulders squared, I vowed then and there that I would be prepared. I would never let him surprise me again. I would watch and catch him. I would show the police I was not hysterical, not delusional, not some flaky young woman.

Once the kids were all down for their naps, I sat at the kitchen table to sip my coffee, staring at the swirly gray pattern of the Formica. I wanted to call my mom and check on her since she was recovering from a broken ankle, but I didn't want to trouble her with what had happened to me. A natural-born worrier, she was also shouldering serious concern about my dad's diagnosis of cancer that had come six months ago. But I did really need to hear her voice.

"Hi, Mom. How's the ankle today? How's Dad?"

"Oh, hi, sweetie. I wondered if you would be too busy to call me today. I'm getting used to your daily calls! Ankle's the same. It's clunking around on these damned crutches that is getting to me. Dad's the same too, which is good. He still doesn't complain, but since he's been back to work, I worry that his strength might be fading. I know the doctor said that almost all patients with this type of cancer of the vocal cords survive, but I can't help worrying. He has a checkup in two weeks, and we will see. What's with you? You sound funny."

"Nothing, really. Just tired."

"Margo, what's up?"

"No, Mom. Nothing."

"Margo?"

"I don't want to bother you, with your ankle and Dad…"

"Margo."

"OK, Mom, OK."

I couldn't help myself. Trying to sound calmer than I felt, I related what had happened the night before.

My father's heritage was German and French, but my mother's was 100 percent Irish. Her entire family—her parents, six siblings, their children and grandchildren—lived on the west side of Grand Rapids, all within a mile of one another. The Irish church and school, Saint James, was across the street from our home and an integral part of the whole family's lives. My aunt and uncle and their nine children lived two houses down from our family of eight. My folks broke my grandmother's heart by moving our family to the east side of town during my senior year of high school. To her, it was as if my father had taken his family across the world and she would never see us again! Funny. Didn't her mother do the same when she left her family in Ireland—crossing an ocean, not just moving across town?

One of my younger sisters, Joni, and I were the closest of friends with two of our impish and fun-loving cousins, Janet and Dori. Growing up, it was always Margo and Janet, Joni and Dori. As kids, we were in all kinds of scrapes and loved make-believe adventures and mysteries.

Around six thirty in the evening, Butch turned off his machine and slid his protective goggles up onto his head. He walked to the breakroom at the plant and found his buddy, Charlie, already seated at their usual table with his usual Nehi grape pop and barbeque chips. His green metal lunchbox was yet unopened. Butch got a bottle of Coke from the machine, took his lunch bag from the shelf, and sat on a folding chair across from Charlie, who said, "Hey, Butch. How's it going?"

"Same old, same old. Number fourteen broke down again, and I could have fixed it in fifteen minutes, but I had to wait for the joker from maintenance to show up and do it. Now I'm behind. Frustrating."

"I hear ya. A couple of guys on my line are so slow, and one guy seems to be off every Friday. It's amazing that we ever meet our quotas. How are ya doin' now with your shop?" Charlie asked.

"Slow but steady so far. It's great being my own boss. You would laugh at my shop. The two grinding machines take up at least half the space. I have a workbench and step stool.

The other day, my oldest boy, Seamus, asked me what my machines do. I told him that a large company manufactures a part, and in the process it gets heat treated. This process enlarges the steel material somewhat, and these parts have to be perfect. When I win the bid, this company sends all the parts to me. Then I grind each piece to the specifications on their blueprint. Sometimes the thickness I need to remove is a lot thinner than this cellophane on my pack of cigarettes. Seamus scrunched up his little nose and just said, 'Oh, funny.'"

"Well, he's a little guy…five, right?"

"Yep. He better hope this shop ends up paying for his college someday."

"Right on. And what's new with Margo and the other kids?"

"Man, I almost forgot. Last night, she saw a peeping tom at our den window. She was pretty hysterical…mostly because the guy didn't move when she opened the curtains. When I got home, the neighbor gal was over."

"Wow. Did Margo call the cops?"

"Yep. Nothing they could do, really. I told her it won't happen again."

Around seven thirty in the evening. I peeked out the window and found that our porch was suddenly crowded with my sisters Joni and Carol Ann; my cousins Janet, Dori, and Geraldine; and my mom, crutches and all. Janet and Geraldine were carrying paper grocery bags. I asked, "Where are your cars?"

Geraldine answered, "We didn't want the prowler to know there were other people here. So we parked them at the end of the street."

"So we're the female version of *77 Sunset Strip*, at your service," announced Janet.

"Except we have no weapons, just food," added Dori.

"Really, you guys, I'm OK."

"Too bad," said Joni. "We're coming in."

Geraldine helped my mom up into the house, and the rest followed, loading BeMo potato chips, Mars candy bars, and Pepsi on the table, taking over my kitchen. Carol Ann, true to form, just looked at me wide-eyed, not saying a word. Leaning against the door jamb, I smiled, grateful for this family of mine. Anne and Danny were asleep. Seamus and Todd had already had their baths, so I finished putting them to bed and joined the gang in the kitchen.

Janet soon declared, "Each of us will take a post and be on duty till Butch gets home from work. We can switch spots after a while, if we want." She loved this stuff. The six of them were stationed around the house, staked out in the dark living room at each window, with Mom sitting in the stairway going upstairs directly across from the front door. I parked in the den with the TV and lights on, just like a normal night. Absolutely nothing happened. Maybe the guy would never return? He probably wouldn't return. Probably.

We later figured that the fact that the glow of a cigarette was in every window could have deterred him. Practiced sleuths we were not. But from then on, we kept our cigarettes low.

Around twelve thirty, Butch came in the front door, looked around at the group, and boomed, "Aha. Margo's posse has arrived. Do you guys really think the weirdo will come back?" The six of them simultaneously babbled their responses, and he threw up his hands. "OK, OK. I'm outnumbered. You being here certainly can't hurt, and I am really happy that Margo had company."

They settled in every night for a week except Saturday and Sunday, when Butch was home. Our nightly pattern was becoming tedious—boring, really—and continued that way until one night around 11:45pm. Dori whispered that a shadow was going down the west-side driveway. No one moved. All was quiet.

Chip, stretched out along the couch skirt, had been sleeping. Suddenly, he leaped up, paced back and forth, and went into a low growl. He raced to the front door, stood on his hind legs, and began pawing the door, barking sharply.

Tiptoeing to the front door (not logical, I knew, as no one could hear me over the loud barking), I opened the door just wide enough to let Chip out. His fur was on end, but he put the brakes on and would not move.

"Come on, Chip; see what's out there."

He was not about to budge. What was that about? Aren't German shepherds supposed to be super watchdogs? This was spooky and disconcerting. Chip, as a line of protection, was not looking so good to me.

My mom said, "Chip knows to stay in the house and protect you, Margo. It's his second nature."

"Really, Mom? I would have thought he would chase after whoever was out there."

"No. Shepherds don't chase. They protect. He was going to stay between you and danger. Good dog!"

We all ended up back in the kitchen, circling the wagons, not saying much. Finally, Janet ventured into the silence.

"Margo, we believed you from the beginning. But then nothing happened for days, and I began to think that there really wasn't a threat anymore. But now...with Chip like a dog possessed and then acting like some kind of protector...I am really scared for you."

"Me too," Joni said. "Why you? Is he a pervert peeping tom or worse?

What does he want? If only we could hide outside."

"No way," chorused Carol Ann and Geraldine.

"We'll figure this out. Tonight could be the end of this, and we could be worrying for nothing," I told them. "Pass me some chips."

Once Butch came home, he checked our backyard, the driveway, and the porch but found nothing out of the ordinary. On the one hand, I was relieved. On the other hand, my intuition told me that this wasn't over. Yet I couldn't expect my family to be here all the time. Butch leaned against the sink, finishing off the bag of chips. The rest of us hadn't moved from the table. My face was now a bright mask of confidence and sincerity.

"All right, everyone," I began. "Nothing really happened tonight or any of the other nights, for that matter. You guys have families and lives, and you can't keep coming over here every night. You've been great, just great. I love and appreciate you all—really I do—but you have to stay home. I'll be fine."

Butch pretty much agreed. "Margo is right, gang. Now get going." He kissed each one as he helped them out the door, down to their cars. As he went around turning off the lights, I put the extra pop in the fridge, blankly staring at its contents and wondering where I would get the courage from now on.

Chapter Four

A Day in the Life Of

I woke up the next day to gray skies and a gray feeling of dread for the evening and darkness to come. My day followed the regular pattern: at seven, I had coffee and ate breakfast with Butch and baby Danny. I cleaned the kitchen and made breakfast for Seamus, Todd, and Anne; vacuumed and washed the crib, windows, and floor in Dan's room; finished three loads of laundry, played with the kids, made lunch for all, and got Seamus ready for his afternoon kindergarten class.

At the shop, Butch was double-checking his orders and invoices and frowning at his disorganization. He knew that for his business to grow, Margo would need to become his unpaid secretary and bookkeeper. He sighed. *Margo is so great with the kids*, he thought, *especially now that I'm not home that much*. He knew he could not make a go of his business without his wife's support. He was very much aware that she was sacrificing a lot for him to realize his dream, but he felt that dwelling on this would do him no good.

Thankfully on Saturday, my Aunt Esther, came over to show me how to setup a chart of accounts. Then she gave me a crash course on bookkeeping.

Butch was thinking to himself that day how nice it will be that all his in-laws would no longer be in his kitchen when he got home each night. What he always looked forward to was hugging his wife and unwinding by cuddling on the couch with her. That was not possible with all those women there. And he did feel that they could have been adding to the hysteria. But he was smart enough not to share any of this with Margo. He understood that she loved the company and was not afraid when they were there. But really, Chip could have been barking at anything, a stray dog or cat or someone just walking by. He really doubted that Dori had seen anything.

Joni walked into General Electric on the corner of Twenty-Eighth Street and Madison Avenue. She didn't even glance at the gleaming new appliances in the showroom as she made her way to her office on the other side of the building. Normally, she would check out the latest shipment of various horse power motors, capacitors, and other parts. But today she was preoccupied with her sister Margo.

Last night, Margo had insisted the family quit coming over to sit with her. She had claimed she was fine, but Joni knew her sister and could still sense her fear and worry. She hung her heavy, charcoal-colored wool coat on the clothes tree, placed her purse in the bottom drawer of the gunmetal-gray desk, and slid into her chair. Joni worked for three engineers, keeping track of orders from major-appliance manufacturers. Alice at the switchboard would be connecting calls to her phone any minute. In two hours, she would walk down the hall to the Coffee Mat vending machine, push the red button for coffee with one cream, and then go back to her desk. Complementing her coffee would be two Girl Scout cookies: Thin Mints. Two hours later, her lunch hour would begin. Today was different, though, as she was consumed with worry for her sister.

My very thoughtful sister, I thought. She had called to say she was on her way with burgers and fries from Fables, a fixture in the neighborhood for years. Their specialty was their deluxe burger with lettuce, tomato, mayo, and sliced green olives, with a side of fresh-cut onion rings, which were deep fried in the restaurant's own distinctive batter. Yum.

In my kitchen, she emptied the bag, and I poured coffee into two Detroit Tigers mugs.

"So," she began, "how are you feeling about tonight?"

"Fine."

"Come on, Margo. At least let me come over tonight."

"No way. Nothing really happened since that one night. It's over. I'm going to live my life just as I did before…and that doesn't include disrupting you and everyone else…as fun as it was having you here." I smiled, but the reality of just thinking about that night, him, the face, the blank stare, the sauntering, the possibility of another encounter, all made me cringe. I carried some dishes to the sink to turn my back on Joni, consciously keeping my body language from betraying my anxiety.

"OK. But promise, promise you will call me if you're scared or just need to talk."

"I will. You're a real sweetheart. And I loved the lunch." We hugged, and she left to return to work.

I watched Seamus, hidden in his burgundy snowsuit, meet his little buddy four houses down and walk off toward school just three blocks away. After I put the little ones in for their naps and shut each bedroom door, my thoughts brought me up short. *Oh my God. These innocent little babies. I have to keep them safe. Should Seamus have walked to school? Is he OK without me?* I breathed heavily. *Now, wait a minute.*

So many children are walking this same path to school. This is broad daylight. Really, Margo. Pull it together. Quit blowing everything out of proportion. Despite this last thought, it took me a while to breathe normally again.

Butch came home later, and I sat with him while he ate his early dinner. I watched him slather butter on a piece of Italian bread and dig into leftover meat loaf and mashed potatoes, and I smiled at his appetite. He kept the conversation light, and we chatted about a new order he was excited about. Finally, he said, "So, honey. Will you be OK tonight alone? I know you're still scared, but there's no way I can't go to work."

"I know. I know. I don't have a choice. I just have to get over this. But it's all so creepy."

"Creepy won't hurt you. You know that."

"You're right. Get to work, and don't worry about me."

After we kissed good-bye and I watched him drive away in our van, I knew I had to counteract this awful powerless feeling or just fall apart. Soon I had a plan. I would be ready, never to be surprised again.

Around five thirty, the kids and I had dinner. As it was already dark, I brought Chip in and put him in the back hall by the driveway side entrance. From this little landing, one could go directly down the basement steps, or up two steps to a half bathroom, or in the door to the kitchen. Chip was secure, and I proceeded to prepare the children for the night. Once they were all in their pajamas, I read them a story and tucked each one in bed, lingering in each room longer than usual.

Once they were all sleeping, I finished the dishes again, finding myself wiping the same raised red-and-green fruit design in the center of the plate over and over again. I picked up the toys scattered everywhere and tossed them into the crates, took the vacuum cleaner out to the back hall, and vac-uumed the dog.

Now it was time for my plan. The stairway opposite the front door of our house was my next destination. I gathered my romance novel, a bottle of Pepsi, the rug, my yarn and crochet hooks, and Chip and climbed to the top to begin my watch. From here I was the guard, perched between the downstairs and my children sleeping behind me. The bare hardwood staircase was not very comfortable, but I didn't plan to move for probably three and a- half hours, until Butch came home.

Around 11:45 the beige princess phone on the nightstand next to our bed rang. Reluctantly I left my post. Chip continued sleeping out in the hall. I sat in the darkness in my bedroom on the ivory chenille bedspread and answered. It was my cousin Dori. The guests from her Tupperware party had just left. She was tired, probably from burping all those lids (our little joke) but could not rest until she spoke with me this first night on my own. We chatted for about ten minutes or so.

Suddenly Chip was in my bedroom pacing back and forth, back and forth. Ignoring him was impossible.

"Margo, what's wrong?"

"Nothing, I hope," I whispered.

Chip charged to the front bedroom window, put his paws on the sill, and emitted a long, deep, continuous snarl. He turned and flew out of the room and down the stairs with an attack growl in his throat. From the edge of my bed, I could hear his paws scraping on the wood front door. This door was a thick, heavy solid oak. The front storm door was shaking. This old wooden storm door had a hook at the top to secure it. I latched that hook every night. When Butch came home, he would try to open the storm door, but the hook held, and the door shuddered from top to bottom. I would then go and let him in. Now the storm door continued its noise.

Dori, still on the line, was screaming, "Margo, are you OK? Do you want me to call the police?"

"I think Butch is home." I was trying to be calm. "But I'm not going downstairs yet. Hold on." I dropped the phone on the nightstand and went to the front window and raised it. I hollered down, "Butch, is that you? *Butch!*" No answer. Chip was still barking. I ran back to the nightstand and picked up the phone. My hand was shaking.

"Dori!"

She yelled, "Margo, don't move! Morey is on his way over to your house. I want you to hang up. Stay right where you are. I'm calling the police. I'll call you right back."

Frozen, I did exactly what I was told. I stood in my dark bedroom waiting for her call. I did not move. So much for my plan to stand watch. My wait for Dori's call seemed like half an hour, but I'm sure only a few minutes passed.

And then there was the comforting ring.

I stayed on the line with her until the flashing red lights flickered through my front bedroom window onto the ceiling. The police pounded on the door. I hung up the phone and skimmed down the steps. Chip was still barking and growling and standing up with his paws on the door. I didn't dare open it because I feared he would mistakenly attack the police. I had to physically carry this large dog to the back hall.

Upon opening the front door, I saw two officers this time, plus Morey, my cousin's husband. They stepped into the hall. The older policeman spoke first.

"Officer Majewski here, ma'am. And my partner, Officer DeVos." I nodded at them. Somewhat composed now, I told them in detail all that had occurred. Majewski said, "You're obviously shook up, ma'am. How can you remember so much?"

"Because my plan is to be ready and somehow catch this guy."

"Really?" He almost chuckled.

"Yes, really. I have four small children here, my husband works nights, and I am not getting help from the police. And—"

"OK. OK. Couldn't it be possible that your dog rattled the storm door? He sounds like a pretty big dog."

"No. Look at this front door! It's thick and solid. Close it right now and try moving that storm door even a little."

"No, no. Not necessary. We'll take your word for it." The younger officer, DeVos, smiled at me. Majewski added, "Don't worry, ma'am. These guys never stay around." They tipped their hats and left.

Mike Majewski, age sixty, and Joseph DeVos, age twenty-five, drove away from the Huver house around twelve thirty in the morning. Majewski glanced at his partner and said, "I haven't worked this shift in a while. Ellison got transferred to narcotics for his rookie rotation. This is the time the broads usually call, and the situation goes nowhere."

"Well, what do ya think happened here? She was just spooked by a noise?" DeVos asked.

"Seems like it. Ya know, sometimes these gals are just lonely. Old man gone. Want to talk to somebody. Sometimes we're just hearing a made-up story. And if anyone is spotted, eyewitness accounts are often way wrong. I can't ever remember catching a peeping-tom type." Majewski sipped his lukewarm coffee.

"But she seemed legitimately upset to me. And she said there was another incident not long ago. You told her these guys never stay around."

"I know. I was just tryin' to make her feel better, Joe. But there was really nothin' we could have done."

"Yeah. And if there was a prowler or peeper, the brother-in-law or whoever he was mighta spooked him."

"True. Time for fresh coffee?"

After the police had left, Morey turned to me and asked, "Aren't they gonna check around the house or somethin'?"

"Nope. They don't do much."

"Well I sure am gonna do something!" He stepped onto the porch, slammed the door, and walked around the house and neighborhood for about twenty minutes, until Butch came home.

Morey met Butch at the door, and I moved closer to hear the whispering.

"I don't know, Butch. Margo was pretty upset and insistent that this front door was being shaken. The police didn't look around. I did—and nothing. I walked around the whole block."

"I don't know what to think either. Margo is very levelheaded, but when it comes to the kids…is she being overly sensitive to noises? She's the only one who hears them. I just don't know."

Wanting to punch them both, I walked toward the front hall. "Excuse me, you two. I am not being too sensitive, and I am not imagining anything! Dori heard everything. Dori called the police. If you could have heard Chip barking and growling and then seen him race to the front door! Really! My sisters and cousins totally believe me."

"It's not that we don't believe you, honey. It's just that it's so frustrating not knowing what is really going on, and me not being able to do anything about it."

Morey added, "Butch is right. If we only had more evidence, maybe the police would listen."

"How am I supposed to get more evidence? I'm not a professional, and the police certainly are not helping." Butch put his arm around my shoulder, but I moved away. I was keyed up, disgusted, hurt, and exhausted, all at the same time.

"Good night, you two."

Across the street, around one thirty in their upstairs bedroom, Jackie Elslander shook her sleeping husband.

"Clarence! Did you hear that?"

"Uh...what? No."

"I heard a noise, a crashing sound. I think on the front porch."

"I didn't. It was probably a cat or something. Let's go back to sleep."

"A cat? A cat wouldn't make that loud of a noise! I'm not kidding."

"All right. All right. I'll go check."

Clarence threw back the red-and-blue patchwork quilt, put on his worn leather slippers, groped for his robe, and walked carefully through their dark bedroom to turn on the hall light. Muttering, he plodded down the stairs, switched on the porch light, and opened the door. The cold night air brushed his fuzzy sleepiness away. Broken glass lay scattered on the front porch. Jackie always put the empty milk bottles by the front door for the milkman to pick up the next morning and replace with their fresh order. One of the bottles had obviously been cracked into five or six pieces.

Clarence peered under the swing and picked up some cigarette butts.

Footprints down the steps and across the lawn were visible too. Clarence glanced around his property but didn't see anything else. Once upstairs, he told Jackie what he had found.

"Pretty odd," he admitted, "but whoever was there is gone now, so don't worry." He climbed into bed and threw his arm over his wife's shoulder.

"You're so cold!" she said.

"No kidding. Let's get some sleep."

Chapter Five

Bring on the Neighbors.
Bring on the Parents.

News of last night's episode spread fast in the neighborhood the next morning. Chris and Marcia came over for coffee by ten o'clock. Marcia and Marv Vandermeer, both thirty-five, and their four children lived directly across the street. Marcia was the neighborhood busybody. Popping into kitchens for coffee or showing up to borrow something kept her in the know on our street. At a neighborhood barbeque, she once announced, "I grew up in the country, and we never had neighbors to socialize with." (Hence her penchant for "neighboring" and gathering tidbits from people's lives.) However, the fact that this woman could fix anything did make her invaluable to us when our husbands were not home. She would stride over dressed in rolled-up blue jeans and an oxford cloth button-down shirt, ready to help. And she was a great source if any of us really needed to know anything.

The two friends were eager for the latest details. No matter the time of day or night, a police car was always noticed and noted. Chris and Marcia wanted to report the chatter of the neighborhood as well as news of their own. I recounted what had happened the night before.

Marcia took a sip of her coffee and then set it down with two hands. Eyes open wide and leaning forward, she began. "You know the people next door to me? Jackie and Clarence? You don't know them well, I understand, but anyway, early this morning, I saw her sweeping her porch. I wondered why she would do that in the winter, so I went to talk to her. Wait till you hear what she told me! Last night, around one thirty in the morning, there was a loud crash out there, and her husband went out to check. You know how we all put our empty milk bottles out on our porches for the milkman? Well, by their front door, Clarence found broken glass. And under their swing were cigarette butts! What do you think of that?"

Chris added, "Margo, your prowler was probably hiding under there, just waiting for the police to leave.

Since the porch can be icy and slippery, he must have tried for a fast exit, slipped, and banged into the milk bottles."

I clasped my hands together and tried not to be too excited.

"Finally, more evidence! I know what I saw that night and what has happened since. Wait till Butch hears this. And I bet my cousin's husband spooked the guy."

"Right," the friends answered in unison.

I got up and grabbed the coffee pot. As I was warming Marcia's coffee, I stopped mid-pour. A prickly cold traveled from my scalp to my toes.

"What's the matter?" she asked.

I looked at both of them.

"The idea of that creep waiting right across the street, watching our house for all those minutes? Who knows? He's probably watching this house and me all the time. Maybe even now!"

"But from where?" Chris asked. "There's really nowhere to hide on our street."

"Not in the daytime," I said. "But at night, he could be any-where. And he can so easily just run down the hill in our back-yards and disappear between those buildings down there." I was beginning to shriek. "Oh my God. I can't take this! I can't even be myself, not even with the kids or with Butch. I don't want any one of the kids out of my sight. I'm mad at Butch for going to work. I'm not getting enough sleep. I—"

Chris took the pot from my hand and gently pushed down on my shoulder until I was sitting. She refilled our cups and suggested, "Maybe we really need a martini."

I couldn't even smile. Would all this get worse? When would it end?

"I'm sorry, Margo," Chris said. "Nothing about this is funny. We have to hope that this guy is just a weirdo peeping tom, that he gets his jollies out of scaring women, nothing more."

"Well, he's certainly succeeded." I put my head down on my folded arms. Both women gently put their hands on my shoulders. There was nothing more to say.

The middle of February was still very cold, and our street remained snow-covered. On February 2, Groundhog Day, the prediction had been for an early spring. I sure hoped for as much. Everything begins over in the spring, and I desperately needed my life to begin again, with this nightmare over.

I was no longer comfortable in the den/dining room once darkness approached. I crowded the television and toys into the living room and moved a table and chairs back to the din-ing room. I only sat in that room in the daytime.

Faithfully, I kept my nightly ritual. At six pm I brought in Chip and vacuumed his whole body, and he was ready for duty watch. I stashed him in the back hall until it was time to go upstairs. From seven to nine was the bedtime ritual. While I bathed Seamus, Todd, and Anne, Dan crawled around the bathroom floor pushing a yellow Tonka dump truck. Once in their pajamas, Seamus and Todd played in their bedroom. Anne, my perfect sleeper, cuddled in my arms for a few minutes and then dove into her bed and hugged her worn blue beanbag doll and closed her eyes. I rocked Danny in the chair near his crib and fed him his bottle, enjoying these moments, for I knew they were fleeting. Soon, he would be drinking from a sippy cup. That night, the boys wanted me to read Curious George. I thought, Please, dear Lord, don't let them become too curious about what's going on.

Once they were in bed, my watch duty began. Three and a half hours perched on the hard second-floor landing each night was very hard on my bottom. To break the monotony and to change positions, I attempted to stand in my bedroom with the lights off. But after staring into the night for several minutes, my eyes would water, and my vision would blur. Reluctantly, I would resume my spot in the hall.

The last known visit from my prowler had been over three weeks ago. But it was impossible for me to become complacent. I still was deathly afraid of his return and was unable to resume normal living. I wanted this dread of mine to be a thing of the past.

One night while preparing to go upstairs with Chip, I saw that the television was still on from Seamus and Todd watching *Zorro.* As I leaned over to turn off the set, one of my favorite shows had just started: *Bonanza.* I thought, *Why not? What difference will an hour make?* My unwelcome visitor never came this early. I luxuriously stretched out on the couch (like a normal person!) to watch the show.

However, bone tired as I was, I promptly fell asleep right after the four Cartwrights rode their horses' right at the screen, with the iconic theme song in the background. I never did witness the three grown sons doing whatever Pa told them to and thus solving the episode's challenge.

My dozing was interrupted as the front door rattled and Chip, from the back hall, began his insistent growling and loud barking. Oh God, no! He's back, and he's early! It's only ten forty five. I couldn't believe our children were such sound sleepers but was so thankful that they were.

Again, the police were called. Yet two different policemen stood on the porch, both with their jackets open and thumbs tucked in their belts. I repeated the litany of the previous calls per their request. Didn't they have records or a file or something? I explained the incident of the neighbors' porch, letting them know that had the police checked around then, the prowler might have been caught. I kept my tone respectful even though I wanted to scream at them.

Joe and Kathryn Wessely were driving away from the Meijer employee awards dinner. Hands on the wheel and looking straight ahead, Joe said, "I'm glad this night air woke me up. That was pretty boring tonight. And it doesn't help that I can only have one drink while on this chemo."

"It wasn't boring last year when you got an award, dear," his wife replied. "Hey Joe, you just turned the wrong way. We're not going toward home."

"I know. I know. I just want to go by Margo's."

"But it's eleven o'clock; she could be asleep. We don't want to scare her."

"I don't care. I just need to go over there."

A car pulled up in front of my house. Both doors swung open and out stepped my parents, my dad in his black overcoat and my mom in her red winter coat with a black fur collar.

I knew they had been to an awards dinner. They had taken a long detour to get to my house.

I greeted them. "You guys, what's up? Why are you here?"

My dad walked right past me and gave it to the officers in his baritone voice. "Why aren't you helping my daughter?"

"There's nothing we can really do, sir" was the answer.

"Does she have to be hurt, or worse, for something to happen? My son-in-law is working at GM, you know, and can't be here to protect her. I sure hope I can catch this idiot. I would like to beat the shit out of him for scaring her and causing everyone all these worries and sleepless nights."

One of the officers gave the stock cop reply of the times: "If you do catch him, sir, be sure to drag him into the house. If you leave him outside, you could be prosecuted for assault."

"You better believe it." My dad moved closer. "Your name, officer?"

"Officer Holt, sir. Stosh Holt." He stood up straighter.

"Well, Officer Holt, make this your priority. I have four little grandkids in that house."

"We will do our best." The other officer was mute and appeared bored. They tipped their hats and walked toward their car.

I called after them, "Don't I even have to sign something this time?"

"Nope. We have your information," the mute officer answered. They slid into their car and drove off, not even giving a cursory look around. Most likely they were on their way to Marge's Donut Shop.

My mom hugged me, and I breathed in the rose perfume that clung to her collar. Seeing her without her crutches was wonderful. I turned to lead my parents into the house, and my dad's strong arm was around my shoulder. I inhaled his

Old Spice cologne, plus a bit of bourbon. The familiarity of their signature scents was a true comfort. We stepped into the house to get out of the cold.

"Do you want us to stay for a while?" my dad asked.

"No, it's not necessary. The guy won't come back. You both have to be up early for work, and I'll be fine. But I think he's probably hiding somewhere. I am sure he's laughing because the police are so useless in this town. And here we are, in the second largest city in Michigan. Pfft! Really, Butch will be home in a few minutes. I'll call you in the morning. Love you guys!"

"OK, honey. We are pretty tired. Now, you try to get some sleep. I just hate this!" my mom said.

"Me too. Me too. Good night, and thanks." My dad held my mom's elbow and helped her down the steps.

The partners of ten years, Stosh Holt and Mark Vitullo, cruised along Division Street. Holt, fair, sandy-haired and hazel-eyed, was short; his five-foot-five frame just made the academy's requirements. Vitullo's hair and eyes were dark brown, melting into his olive complexion. He towered over most, at six feet five inches. Mutt and Jeff jokes had dogged them for years, but they were a respected team.

"That was a pretty easy call for the beginning of a weekend," Holt said.

"Yeah," Vitullo said. "If the old man wouldn't have shown up, it would have even been easier. And he probably scared the lady even more."

"Weekends are usually more exciting than this. That's why I don't mind taking this extra shift once in a while. And the extra money helps."

"No kidding, Stosh. I was talking with my grandpa, and when he started on the force in 1925 he only made $2250.00 and brings that up anytime I bitch about my salary.

Say, what do you think about the neighbors who found that stuff under their porch swing?" "Could easily have been the same guy. But what are we supposed to do about it? Match a cigarette butt to every schmo who smokes in this town?"

As my parents drove away, I closed and locked the door. I turned and leaned against it, at first berating myself. I couldn't believe I had fallen asleep at nine I should have been on my self-imposed sentry duty! And then fear and loneliness crept in. My hope for help from the police had faded to nil. *And how does this man know when I'm off guard? He only shows up when I'm alone. Where is he hiding? What does he want?* Slowly, I climbed the stairs, sat in my spot, and stroked the back of Chip's neck.

My life was now regulated like a prisoner's. I didn't dare hire any young-girl babysitters anymore because I didn't want them scared or hurt, to say nothing of my children. I smiled as I thought about some Saturdays in the past. Sometimes, if Butch had to work on a weekend, we hired a babysitter for our "date," which consisted of me joining him at the shop. The workspace had a phone on the wall, a combined step stool with a seat, a workbench, and two machines. The filing and bookkeeping I did at home. At the shop, I was happy running a grinding machine. Ah...precious time alone without the children. This was a real thrill at the time. Always my treat would be to get a burger at the Red Rocket or the Elbow Room. And now that simple yet important thrill had been taken from our young lives. My smile turned into a sigh and a heavy heart.

Butch pulled his van into the long line of vehicles leaving the plant. Each night, a policeman directed traffic so the afternoon shift people could get out on the road and head for home. Quite a few guys did not head home but drove half a mile to the Jax Bar for a couple of longnecks. *Maybe before Margo and the kids*, Butch often thought, *but not now.* What about the last two episodes? If the guy across the street who broke the bottles was the same one, then he probably wasn't just bugging Margo but was looking into other houses too. Somehow, that made the guy seem less threatening. And Chip barking at the front door? Did the dog sense Margo's fear, making him super sensitive to noises? Butch didn't know. The fact that the police once again hadn't found anything made him feel a little better.

Butch chuckled at the account of his father-in-law giving the cops the what-for. He loved his in-laws and knew they were protective of their daughters. It really bothered him to think that Margo's parents could feel he was neglecting his family, but just what was he supposed to do?

Butch and I did feel comfortable hiring my neighbor's son, Jimmy Martinez, who was strong and husky. A busy college freshman, Jimmy was on the wrestling team, and he was not always available. We were very selective and only asked him to babysit on very important occasions. The result was that when I would have normally hired a sitter, I now took all four children with me. Doctor appointments were an adventure. One time, the three oldest kids and I needed polio shots and the baby a booster shot. In the sparse, pea-green waiting room, my four were all over the place, not interested in the toys in the diaper bag but more in crawling under chairs, tossing outdated, worn magazines on the floor, and staying out of my reach. Wouldn't you think this office would have a play area or something? One woman glared at me over her copy of *Redbook.* Another smiled sympathetically. I was perspiring, and my bouffant flip was losing its bouffiness---apparently not enough Aqua Net.

Once in the exam room, the three children froze, and the nurse frowned and left, soon returning with two more nurses. They were aware, as I was, that after the first shot was administered, all would be crying. Four children, four shots...done amid much wailing. My shot hurt like hell, but I wasn't about to wail! That day, I napped along with the children.

Grocery shopping was a joke. Seamus, a normal five-year-old full of piss and vinegar, pushed the shopping cart with his little sister, Anne, in the front. He steered in a serpentine manner, annoying the other customers and once knocking over a display of Velveeta cheese. Behind him, I pushed another cart with baby Dan in the infant seat as I hung onto Todd's chubby three-and-a-half-year-old hand. Rarely did all items on my list make it into the basket, and often when putting the groceries away, I would find strange items not on my list. *Hemorrhoid cream? A potato peeler? Another package of Oreos?* And I was lucky to go through the checkout line without a child pilfering a candy bar, another crying, and another having to go to the bathroom. Getting food into our house was an exhausting field trip. An absolute special treat was when Butch got home early enough on a Saturday for me to go shopping all alone. Grocery shopping became my time alone, my salvation, and I cheerily went up and down the aisles, looking at everything. Pretty sad, I thought. I often remarked how I would love it if stores were open on Sundays.

Chapter Six

A Night Out

I could not believe it. A real celebration! A night out! Wow! We were actually going out for dinner *and* dancing the following Saturday night at the credit union's annual celebration, and we only had to pay for drinks. We confirmed that Jimmy could babysit and were so happy to be confident and comfortable with him. And Seamus and Todd were excited. I'll bet they looked forward to a change in the routine too. Anne and the baby continued to be happy and oblivious little ones. Lucky them.

One morning, Chris and I rounded up the young troops and ventured to the resale shop. I really wished I could afford Herpolsheimer's, but I couldn't just yet. Anne and Dan sat in the stroller next to me while I searched the racks for a complement to my black silky skirt at home. Within seconds, Seamus and Todd dove under a circular rack of women's slacks to hide. Chris played along until Todd yanked a few pairs off their hangers. Then she grabbed their hands and went to search out the toys at the other end of the store.

Flipping through a crowded rack of mostly dowdy tops, I stopped at a very pretty yellow Neiman Marcus blouse with ruffles on the cuffs, quite dressy, for only a dollar. It looked as if it had never been worn. A single dollar for a fancy

department-store blouse. What a find! And sitting in my closet gathering dust was the perfect pair of sexy black pumps to
go with it. Pushing the stroller, I negotiated the aisles, a maze
of items from clothes to lamps to bedding, and followed delighted squeals to arrive at the toys. Seamus was waving a
thick, brand-new cowboy coloring book and box of sixty-four
Crayola crayons. Todd pushed a red metal train engine along
the slate-gray industrial carpet. Chris was holding Raggedy
Ann and Raggedy Andy dolls for the two little ones. She said,
"My treat. My kids are too big for stuff like this. And I can
cough up a few bucks."

"Chris, you are great. Kids, what do you say?"

"Thank you."

"Thank you."

"And Chris, look at this beautiful blouse! It's Neiman
Marcus. Ta-da!"

"Perfect and so pretty. Also, Margo, you can use my sparkly evening purse. And let's check out a few of my necklaces."

"Great. Thanks! Butch and I are so excited. Just think.
We're going out like a normal couple."

As we walked to the car, I put my arm around Chris, my
sanity savior. The three oldest kids scampered into the back
seat, and I held Dan on my lap for the ride home.

Finally, Saturday arrived. While the babies were napping
and Seamus and Todd were parked in front of the television
set watching weekly cartoons, I found time to sneak in a long-
deserved bubble bath. No quick in-and-out shower for me today. The bubbles crackled around my ears as I sank low into
the soothing hot water. Delicious.

Butch had promised he would get home early, but, as
usual, he worked right up to the very last minute. The event
started at six, and I didn't want to miss anything. I had laid out

his clothes on our bed. When he arrived home, he ran up the stairs and breezed into the bedroom.

"I just need to take a fast shower and shave, and I'll be ready to go. Don't worry. We won't be too late."

The children had all had their dinner, and the dishes were washed and the kitchen cleaned. Chip had been vacuumed and was in the back hall. While Butch showered, I carefully got ready and went downstairs to let Jimmy in. I looked up at him as he took the black scarf off his thick neck and tossed his blue-and-gold letter jacket on the stairs.

He had no idea how important he was to us. Seamus and Todd stood shyly behind me for a bit, but toddler Anne hugged Jimmy's knees. Dan was in the playpen gumming a squeaky toy.

When Butch finally came down, I was in the kitchen. He stood there smiling at me.

"Wow! You look fantastic. How much did that fancy outfit cost? I'm in this six-year-old suit!"

I replied, "Oh, this new blouse is way within our budget."

He grabbed me and held me close, and we spun around the tiny kitchen, our corner of heaven right then. We kissed the kids good-bye, got into the van, and just looked at each other. Alone. Out of the house and on the town.

I'm sure that as we walked into the event hall, my eyes were as wide and shimmery as they had been on our wedding day. The crystal chandeliers and elegantly set tables reflected my sparkle. Two vodka gimlets before dinner, and I was happily relaxed and thrilled to be served my meal. I savored the steak while it was still hot—no stopping to cut meat for a small one or wipe up spilled milk. I couldn't stop smiling, and relishing un-interrupted adult conversation was a holiday unto itself. Door prizes were awarded. No, we didn't win. That was fine, as our prize was just being able to walk in the door.

The live band started at nine, with the usual fox-trot hits from the forties. We dreamily danced to Old Blue Eyes and were on the floor through fifties rock and roll, Motown, and Elvis. We only sat down for the twist, a dance popular when I was very pregnant with Todd and never mastered. I guess I couldn't make my hips move correctly. Late in the night, the lead singer had almost convinced us he was Paul Anka for the last song: "Put Your Head on My Shoulder." An absolutely superb night—I was Cinderella at the ball. But Cinderella's magic night had to end.

We arrived home around one in the morning, tired but very, very happy. Our smiles disappeared when we saw the expression on Jimmy's face.

"Jimmy, what's wrong? Did the children get hurt?" Butch asked.

I was afraid to speak, and my knees were weak.

"No! No! Kids are fine, all sleeping fine. But we had a visit from your prowler! That sure scared me skinny! I was very good to Seamus and Todd tonight. I let them stay up way past their bedtime and made them popcorn, and we were watching *Gunsmoke* when Chip began to growl, really mean, from the back hall. At almost the same time, the front storm door shook. I ran to the front-room window and pulled back the drapery, and I saw this man standing on the porch. He saw me, and I just froze...that spooky face and beady eyes with a strange kind of flat look just staring at me! I didn't want to scare the boys, so I acted like nothing was wrong, but I almost peed my pants. Really! I called the cops and gave the boys more popcorn."

My chest tightened, knowing what he had experienced—and to think we hadn't been home with for children!

Jimmy spoke faster now.

"Waiting for them to arrive seemed like a long time, but it was probably not more than ten minutes." He sat on the edge of the couch, elbows on his knees, his huge hands opening and closing.

"When they finally got here, I stepped out on the porch to talk to them in private, so the boys wouldn't hear. Either Seamus or Todd slammed the front door shut, and it automatically locked me out. That was embarrassing. I felt like a real jerk. I shouted, 'Seamus! Open the door!' over and over. They laughed, but they wouldn't open the door. Those two are imps. The cops helped me jimmy the front dining-room window, which looked like it was locked, but the latch hadn't caught. We got it open, and I climbed in. One cop asked me a few more questions, and then they left. I'm really sorry about all this. I can't believe how scared I was. What's with that guy?"

"Jimmy," I said, "nothing is your fault here. You did all the right things. And if this wasn't so awful and frightening, this whole scene tonight would be funny."

"Not laughing yet."

"OK, Jimmy. Try to remember. What exactly did this guy look like?"

"I don't know. I was so shocked and scared. He had that dark hair, and those dark, weird eyes with that kinda empty look."

"Did he have on a hat? What was he wearing? What about his skin color? How tall was he? Did you tell the cops anything about him?"

Butch said, "Honey, slow down. Give him a chance. All right, Jimmy, tell us anything else you can."

"He wasn't wearing hat. I don't know about his skin color. Um…don't know what he was wearing. I just stared at his face for a few seconds. I couldn't move. Then he left. I looked down at him, so he musta been shorter than me. That's all I know. Sorry. I just can't believe how shook I was. Really, I was a wimp. And, yes, I told everything to the cops."

"There's nothing to be sorry about," I said. "But what about the boys? Did they talk to the cops? Were they scared?"

"No. I told them the policemen wanted to talk about a bunch of bikes that were stolen. I asked if they wanted to take their popcorn and some books up to their room and said I would be up soon. They grabbed their bowls and were up the stairs in no time, giggling away. I was afraid they would wake the other two."

"Good job. We're so lucky you were our sitter," Butch told Jimmy as he handed him his money. "Get on home now, and get some sleep."

"Thanks, Mr. Huver. Sure hope they catch this guy. Let me know."

"Will do." Butch shook his hand and then helped him on with his jacket.

Jimmy raised his shoulders and lowered his chin against the frosty night. *I still can't believe how I wigged out*, he thought. *It had to be that weird stare on that guy's face. And those little brats! You'd think the cops would have a tiny bit of a sense of humor. Nope. At least Mr. and Mrs. Huver understood and weren't mad at me. I hope, anyway.*

He stomped the snow from his feet in the tiny vestibule of his house and hung his jacket and scarf in the front closet. His dad was slumped asleep in his favorite armchair. Vertical stripes in primary colors were on the TV screen, as there was no more programming on that channel until morning. Jimmy walked up to the blond-wood television console and turned the set off. His dad stirred and blinked his eyes at Jimmy for a moment. "Oh, hi, son. I guess I dozed off." Once clear-eyed, he asked, "Jimmy? What's the matter? You OK?"

"No. Yes. Now I am." He sank into the hunter-green velour couch and told his father all the details of the evening.

"You know," his dad commented, "I really thought Margo was exaggerating or a little hysterical about all this. But now we know she's for real. You did all the right things, and everyone is safe, including you. How are the Huvers?"

"Shook up. That's for sure. But they were happy I was their sitter and were really nice to me."

"That's what I would expect of them. They're good people. Let's hope that guy stays away from our street. All right, let's hit the hay."

Jimmy stood up, thinking, *I am really beat, but I'm not sure I can sleep.*

Holt and Vitullo had driven around the block and down into the industrial area to look around for anyone at all.

"Here we are takin' extra duty again on a Saturday night. And we're called to the same house," said Holt. "My wife is not too happy about me working tonight, cuz we were supposed to play euchre with her folks. But geez, she doesn't mind the extra cash!"

"Linda's fine with me working more, seeing as we have number three coming in about six months," Vitullo said.

"Holy smokes! What's that? Three kids under four now, with the new one? Haven't you figured out what causes this?"

"Very funny. But truthfully, we gotta make this the last one. Linda should find out about this new pill. Boy, Stosh, this spot is really deserted and dark. The guy could easily disappear here, even if we were chasing him on foot. How funny was that big galoot babysitter? He was really spooked, mostly because he saw the peeper's face, I guess."

"The damn little squirts locking the door didn't help either. Let's cruise around the main streets. The guy's long gone from this neighborhood. Let's see if we can spot a short guy with dark hair."

Vitullo laughed. "Cuz that's enough to stop him for!"

After Jimmy left, I finally took off my coat and slipped off my heels. Butch sat with me on the couch, his arm around me. All sorts of thoughts were crowding our heads.

Butch spoke first. "This was the first Saturday this guy showed up. Normally, I'm home on Saturday nights."

"Right," I added. "But tonight we were out, and our white van was not here."

The fact that the prowler had come while Jimmy was baby-sitting was both terrifying and lucky. The creep had not gotten in the house, and no one was hurt. And now someone else had seen him! I guessed that part was good. I would gain some credibility. I was not overreacting—or worse, making things up. The questions remaining in my head, of course, continued to be the same. What did that face in my window want, and why?

Later, Butch got out of bed and stood looking out the window onto the street below. The trees' shadows on the snow from the streetlights looked sinister to him. He allowed all the fearful thoughts to play in his head. A new wrinkle—no, more than a wrinkle—had entered the picture. Someone else had actually seen this guy. Jimmy, a college kid. Not a hysterical twelve-year-old girl. And Jimmy had certainly been scared.

Butch thought about the kids. Seamus and Todd had been just a few feet away from this man, this intruder in their lives—maybe even a real criminal. He swore under his breath. *We don't have an extra penny to hire someone to stay with Margo when I'm out. And would that do any good?* Quitting his job or giving up on the shop were not options she would agree to.

He pictured a scene where the guy got into the house. According to his wife and now Jimmy, this man was small and slight. Surely, Chip would attack. He would tell Margo never to leave the dog penned on the back landing after dark. Butch sighed and slumped his shoulders. The next second, he straightened them. He remembered that the foreman at the plant had a brother on the police force. He would talk to him as soon as he could. He crawled back into bed, slid next to Margo, and with at least a plan in his head, he went right to sleep.

Chapter Seven

Endless Nights and Episodes

My daily moods were now on a bell curve. Upon waking, I would realize that nothing had changed regarding my stalker. Sometimes I fantasized about keeping my bedroom dark; piling heavy covers on top of me, and slipping back to sleep. But soon, Anne and the baby would wake up, and Seamus and Todd would join us in my bed. Cuddles and giggles would quickly lift my funk. After breakfast, I was busy reading more and more now to sweet Anne while Dan bounced on my knee. Seamus and Todd entertained each other with their miniature cowboys and Indians. Soon Seamus was off to school, and the other three took naps. All was wonderful in their worlds. I would clean up and maybe read the paper.

Butch would come in, change his clothes, and sit down for his afternoon dinner. He would leave, and the little ones' naps were over just as Seamus pounded on the front door. I would check Seamus's "artwork" and notices from the school. Diapers were changed, and I thought about our dinner. Then the gloom started as I knew I had to face the night again. Once Butch left for General Motors, I was on my way back to my early-morning funk; only now it was evening, and I was at the bottom of the curve.

So many long nights found me sitting on the hard floor in the upstairs hall with my faithful Chip. I listened. I watched for any quick movement from the dog. I then moved to my bedroom window and peered out at the darkened street. When Chip didn't move, I was back to the hall. I read four books over the next several days and finally finished the rug I was crocheting. I was amazed at how cozy this homemade addition made the living room, except I didn't have the luxury of allowing myself any coziness. I would picture the unfinished rug flying off my lap and still heard the *ding, ding, ding* of the metal crochet hook on the hardwood floor. The image would change to that frozen face inches away from mine on the other side of the window pane.

One evening, Chris and Marcia rang the doorbell.

"Just wanted to come over for a bit," Marcia said.

"Yep," Chris added, "just over for my favorite…a Coke and a smoke." They plopped onto the dining room chairs, and soon we were chatting away.

Marcia had bumped into Mrs. Cracco at Meijer.

"She said she was sure she saw a man on her back porch the other night, but when she double checked, he was gone. The old lady was really in a dither."

"Really?" I said. "Maybe the old battle-ax was strutting in her bathing suit in the backyard this summer, and the guy couldn't resist another peek?"

"Right on!" Chris laughed.

About an hour later, a huge bang sounded from the kitchen. Simultaneously, we all leaped up, screaming and running for the front door, the three of us banging into one another. Chris and Marcia ran outside, and I stood by the door. Hysteria set in on the front lawn, and Marcia ran for Marv.

"I'm freezing out here," Marcia said.

"Well, I'm not going back in there!" Chris yelled.

I needed to stay in the house for my kids, so I just held the door open. Marv ran over, and with courage in numbers, we went inside and into the kitchen. Sitting on the floor was Todd, eating a graham cracker.

"I'm hungry, Mommy. Are you mad?"

"No. No, sweetie." I got down on the floor and cuddled him. "Just come find me and tell me you're hungry from now on, OK?" He had never woken up in the middle of sleep before, much less come downstairs. I carried his warm, soft body back upstairs, and he was asleep immediately.

We adults reconvened in the living room, relieved and chagrined.

"Oh my gosh," I said. "That was just like an episode of *I Love Lucy* or *Dick Van Dyke*."

"We are just so on edge that we act crazy," Chris said.

"Tell me about it," I said. "Once again, thanks for all the help. Go on home now, and I'll talk to you guys tomorrow." After they all left, I wearily climbed up the stairs to my spot, leaned my head against the wall, and fell asleep.

Spring finally arrived. Night duty was more difficult because the snow no longer provided a contrast to the objects outside my windows. The loneliness of my watch at my bedroom window was compounded at eleven thirty each night as my neighbors' lights went out and their homes melted into the darkness. I couldn't help but begrudge them being safely tucked in for the night as I strained my eyes, searching the neighborhood landscape for any sign of him. The last hour and a half of my watch was always more difficult and scary. But my unwelcome visitor had not bothered me in two weeks.

The fresh spring air and the freedom of being outside was wonderful. One Sunday afternoon, we pulled out all the old overgrown bushes from the front of our house and planted new little elder bushes and some hardy, deep-pink peonies and purple Russian sage. They looked a bit puny now, but by midsummer, they would be lush and lovely. I was successful that day at almost totally squashing my dread of nights awaiting me.

Monday morning, Butch left for the shop very early, as he had to make up for all the time he had spent working on the yard over the weekend. At six o'clock, I flopped across our bed, waiting to hear Danny, and quickly fell sound asleep. Danny, our happy, perfect baby, didn't wake that morning until almost eight thirty, when I heard his cute babbling from the room across the hall.

I was in his bedroom changing his diaper when the front door slammed shut. *Oh my God! Oh my God! Did the prowler get in? It's so early. It's daytime, my safe time.* Grabbing Dan, I ran to the children's bedroom. Seamus and Todd were not in their beds. *Oh my God! Did he take them?* I rushed to the front window. My boys were walking down the sidewalk, all dressed up in their Sunday best—red blazers, black dress pants, white shirts and ties, their churchgoing clothes. *What's going on?* I quickly woke up Anne, charged down the stairs, carrying both little ones, and flew out the front door. I hollered, "Seamus! Todd! *Stop!*"

Seamus seemed perplexed.

I asked, "What's going on? Where are you going?"

Seamus said, "I'm bringing Todd for show-and-tell today. Mrs. Armstrong said we could go to the morning class and bring something very special that makes us happy. I'm bringing Todd."

What? I thought. I didn't remember seeing a note for that in his stack of papers.

"Well, Seamus, that's very nice, but you do have to ask permission from your father and me. You can't just leave home without talking with your parents to make sure it's OK with them."

"Mommy, you might say no!"

"Sorry, Seamus. That's the breaks. Sometimes it's yes. Sometimes it's no. You always have to check with your parents. Promise me you will never do anything like this again. Always, always talk about things you would like to do."

"I promise, Mommy. I'm sorry. I'm really sorry."

"If I hadn't seen you down on the sidewalk, I would have thought you were missing. I would have cried all day."

Both little guys were getting teary.

"Well, everyone's up. Let me get dressed, and we'll all walk you to your show-and-tell day."

Butch had a great laugh when I told him that story and about the scene in the kitchen with Todd. By this time, I was really able to laugh about those two on a mission and Marcia and Chris yelling out on the front lawn.

After those escapades, the next days were smooth and productive. I spent most of my time outside in the sunshine with the children. Spring weeding and yard cleanup gave me some tired muscles.

One Thursday evening after the normal routine, I turned on *I Spy*. The controversial show starred Bill Cosby and Robert Culp, a black man and a white man teaming up. I loved that show. I lay down on the couch to enjoy it, but of course I was soon sound asleep. Next thing I heard was Butch at the front door, and tonight he woke me. Yes, the storm door rattled, but Chip didn't growl or bark at all.

Soon, Butch was sitting at the small table in the breakfast nook just off the kitchen and reading the *Grand Rapids Chronicle* while I warmed up pasta and meatballs and toasted some bread for him.

"Man, what a day," he said. "Two guys called in sick at the plant, and one of the machines at the shop is giving me fits. I'm glad to be home now in the peace and quiet."

"Boy, Butch, I must have really been out. I didn't even hear your van in the driveway."

"That's because the van wouldn't start. Charlie drove me home. He tried to give me a jump start, but no go. He'll try again in the morning when he can actually see what he's doing."

"Here's hoping. That old white thing needs to last longer."

"Amen to that!"

I cleared the table and just piled the dishes in the sink this time. Butch returned to reading the paper, and I headed for the couch. Ahh, Butch was home. No aches and pains from sitting on the floor for me! I was content, finally relaxed and happy.

Suddenly, Chip went into his growling and loud barking mode. Again there was the sinking in my stomach, the shortness of breath. *He's back.* I tried to get up but had no strength in my legs. All I could do was roll from the couch to the floor and crawl, yes, down on my hands and knees, from the living room into the kitchen past Butch sitting at the table.

"Margo! Margo, honey! What the hell? My God, Margo. Get up. I'll help you."

I was already at the kitchen door, reaching up to open the door to the back hall. "Chip! Chip! Come!" He was standing on his hind legs, his front paws clawing up high on the side door to the driveway. He was looking out through its window, barking with intermittent long, deep growls. The dog had been sleeping for five hours, but he was wild now and would not come out into the kitchen. Butch was right behind me. He had never seen our dog act like this before.

"Oh my God. Now I really know what you've been talking about!" In a few seconds, Butch turned and ran to the front hall, hollering, "Lock this door behind me! I'm going to find the bastard and make him wish he never bothered you!"

I did as he asked and left the door to the kitchen open. Chip quieted down, lying down by the side door to guard it. I knew that calling the police would be futile. Butch was out there searching. Surprisingly, I was not afraid for him. He would search the whole neighborhood, and the prowler might meet his match tonight.

Fifteen minutes passed. Then Chip was back at it, up on his hind legs and growling, paws on the wooden door, watching out the window. Before I could react, Butch was calling and knocking at the front door. *Thank you, God.*

"I checked the entire neighborhood," he reported, "both sides of the street, down the sidewalk. Checked every driveway, came back through the backyards. The second I put one foot on our driveway, Chip started going nuts again. This dog is a keeper." He came closer, put his arms around me, and said, "Margo, tomorrow I am buying you a gun."

I sucked in my breath. "Right. If I had a gun, I might have shot Todd that day. No way! I do not want a gun. I have never touched a gun. They scare me. No! No way!"

"You do realize that this guy thought you were alone because the van was not in the driveway. You were crazy scared, honey. I saw that tonight. Let's just think about—

"Nothing to think about. No gun. We'll have to figure something else out."

Butch couldn't believe his wife fell asleep so fast. *But then again*, he thought, *with everything she had to do all day, plus me not being around, plus the stress of this maniac prowler, it's no wonder she crashed into sleep.* He couldn't get to sleep, though. His buddy at the plant had said his cop brother wouldn't offer much help. Apparently, the officers filled out cards about the prowler complaints and threw them in a box— end of story. Unless the peeper was caught on or near the premises, nothing could be done.

And a gun? God. The idea of her with a gun in her hand— or needing a gun—or a gun in the house with the kids! If I'd stopped and thought about it, I would have known she would have no part of the idea. But what else could be done? He faced the fact that nothing could, except moving away.

Chapter Eight

Fingerprints and Footprints

The next day, we woke up to a beautiful spring morning with the sun shining, a bright blue sky, and a cool breeze. Out the kitchen window, a brilliant cardinal and his not-so-brilliant mate perched in the soon-to-be-flowering crabapple tree. This kind of day made me feel like singing and warmed my heart. Knowing that Butch truly believed me also warmed my heart. He had witnessed the frantic sounds of Chip and had been horrified at me reduced by fear to being unable to walk and crawling on the floor. "We'll figure this out; we'll figure this out," he had whispered to me the night before as we fell asleep.

After breakfast, we took our second cups of coffee and little Danny out in the yard. Charlie was going to pick up Butch soon to go tinker with the van. "Let's walk around and check out your new plantings," Butch said. He didn't appreciate flowers the way I did, but he knew how much I loved gardens. "Oh no!" he exclaimed. "Shit! I can't believe this."

Our house was forty years old, and all the construction was original. The wooden storms and screens were held in place with hook-type latches at the top and secured with wing nuts on each of the lower sides. Near one of the living-room windows were footprints sunk into the damp soil, and the wing nuts had been released so that one of the storms could swing open. Large muddy thumbprints stood out beside each wing nut. Worse was that the inside living-room window had been raised four or five inches.

"Oh! No, no!" I gasped. "Oh, God help me. He almost got in! Our babies!"

Butch hollered, "Call the police! They can check the fingerprints. Maybe they can catch him."

Just then, Charlie pulled up and ambled toward us in the backyard. He was tall and lanky and seemed to be working on the Beatles look with his brown hair. A cigarette dangled from his mouth, the smoke gently blowing behind him. "What's going on?"

I was holding back tears, so Butch told him what we had discovered.

"Let me see," said Charlie. Hands shoved in his pockets, Charlie followed Butch to the window.

"Holy smokes!" He crushed his cigarette butt out in the grass. "Here's evidence if I've ever seen it."

We all went inside. I shooed Seamus and Todd away from the TV and upstairs to get dressed. They didn't need to hear the phone call. Anne was playing on the kitchen floor with her doll. Butch made the call and explained the situation, but he was put on hold. He stood there fuming.

Charlie said, "Buddy, we have to get going to work on your van. I only have an hour or so."

"Just go, you guys. I can handle this." I put Danny down and took the phone from Butch. Anne squealed as Danny crawled toward her doll.

"OK, honey. But lock the doors. I'll be home as soon as I can. God, I hate this."

"I know. But he doesn't show up in the daytime, and lots of neighbors will be outside today."

Butch kissed me good-bye while I was still on hold, and they left. Finally, I reached the right department. I briefly related the history of the prowler and now the attempted break-in, the footprints, and the visible thumbprints. I told them we needed an officer to check out the prints. The response? "Lady, we can't take prints from wood." Really? I couldn't believe that was true. They really didn't care. They wouldn't take me seriously.

"Man." Sergeant Bird hung up the phone and smoothed out his graying mustache with his thumb and index finger. "That lady wanted us to come get muddy fingerprints off wood from her window. Didn't seem to believe me that it's not possible. She was pretty ticked."

"Ya know," said Lieutenant Reilly, leaning against Bird's desk with his freckled arms folded, "even if we could, lotsa luck getting any help. My cousin Patrick is a cop in Chicago in the Back of the Yards neighborhood. Murders. Gangs. Drugs. Serious stuff all the time. He says they're lucky to get an evidence technician to even help them out. There just aren't enough of those guys. And that's big-time Chicago, not Grand Rapids. Ya gonna fill out a card?"

"Nah. Nothing to report."

No one from the police department came over that day. I decided *never* to call them again! It was time for a new plan. I called Chris and Marcia to come for coffee, to get their thoughts. By the time the fresh pot was ready, they were parked at the front door. I took them out to the yard and pointed out the window, at the muddy footprints and the thumbprints.

Marcia, shocked, turned to me. "You called the police, right? What did they say?"

"Said they couldn't get prints off wood, and that was that."

"Wait a minute." Chris frowned. "The police are here to help us."

"That's what I used to think. Not anymore. Face it. I'm alone in this except for you guys and my family."

Marcia was livid. "That is unacceptable. I can't believe this. I mean, really—"

I broke in. "I have an idea, what I need is your opinion. What if I would call some men in the neighborhood if I need help when Butch is at work? I would like a few names so I'm not bugging the same guys all the time. I certainly don't want the wives mad at me! The men right here on our street might be able to see or catch this guy. This is all I have right now."

"Good idea," Marcia said. "Marv isn't afraid of anything. I'll check with him tonight."

"Thanks. That'll be such a relief. Chris, don't tell Andy. His high blood pressure and heart problems don't need this. And you've been a rock for me."

"I have to agree about Andy. He never even woke up that first night you called me. But there are other guys to call. I'm sure Dick and Cornell would be willing to help if you needed them."

By that evening, I had chosen my defense team: Marv, Dick, and the Salvation Army minister, Cornell. On Monday night, I sat on the edge of our bed and with the address book on my lap, I began dialing. Marv, being tall and strong yet gentle, offset Marcia with his tact. "Hey, Margo. Marcia gave me the lowdown. No problem. When you need me, you call me. At first, I thought Marcia was exaggerating. Know what I mean?" Luckily, he couldn't see my smile. "But now I get it. Tell Butch he can count on me too. I'm ready."

"Thanks so much, Marv. I do so much better with a plan. I really, really appreciate your help."

Next, I called Dick Martinez. He and Roseanne were forty, and besides Jimmy, they had a son, Michael, thirteen. Dick was fiery and fun and always let the young kids climb all over him. Roseanne, an Italian war bride, was a bit reserved and unsmiling. She seemed sometimes to disapprove of how I handled the kids. That was my perception, anyway. I explained the situation and my request.

Dick replied, "After what happened when Jimmy babysat, I thought Roseanne called you about it to check on you." Nope, she hadn't. "Of course, I'll be available. Don't give it another thought. This wacko prowler will be sorry if he sees me! And I know Butch would help us out if we needed him."

He'd have to be home to do that, I thought. "Great, Dick. I feel so much safer already."

I hesitated before dialing Cornell McGregor. He was a roly-poly guy of about fifty, with college-age boys and a daughter, a son-in-law, and two grandkids just north of Detroit. I didn't know him and his wife, Sarah, very well, but he had always been friendly enough.

"Hello, Cornell? This is Margo Huver."

"Yes, Margo. Hi. I heard about what's been going on. Must be awful scary for you without Butch home."

"For sure. That's why I'm calling. I may need a favor."

"Anything."

"Well, the police haven't been able to help at all in looking for or catching this prowler. I would like to be able to call you if he shows up at my house, or if I see him near yours or something, when Butch is gone at night. Marv and Dick will be available, too, so it shouldn't be too often and, God willing, not at all."

"Of course. Of course. My goodness. My job is about helping all kinds of people. I'd better be able to help out a neighbor. Don't you worry. And I'll pray for you and your family too."

Cradling the phone on my lap, I felt satisfied.

A few nights later around eleven, I had fallen asleep sitting in the upstairs hallway, my head hanging down and my body leaning to one side, when the phone rang. I stumbled into my bedroom and grabbed the receiver. "Hullo?"

"Margo, it's me, Roseanne. We just heard someone running between our house and the McGregor's. Dick is after him."

I slammed the phone down and hurried to the window. Dick, in his pajamas and slippers, was wielding a machete. What in the world? He disappeared around the side of our house, headed toward the backyard. Of course, Chip was barking away now—but was it about the prowler or Dick or both? I threw Butch's Detroit Lions sweatshirt over my nightgown, grabbed Chip's collar, and carefully ventured into the yard.

I met Dick as he trudged up the hill from the direction of the industrial area below. The machete at his feet, he was out of breath and bent over with his hands on his thighs. He struggled to talk. By now, Chip was wagging his tail and happily circling Dick.

"I saw him! I saw him! Couldn't catch him. He was always forty yards ahead.

Dammit! Dammit! Dammit!"

"Hey, come on in the house. Let's sit down." In the kitchen, I handed him a glass of water. "Dick, did you get a good look at him?"

"Not really," he said. "It's so dark, and he was really moving. He had dark pants and a dark jacket, I guess. Short for a man. Sorry. Sorry."

"Dick, don't worry about it. You probably saved me another huge fright, and I wasn't alone for a change. What a difference. But what's with the machete, for Pete's sake?"

"My uncle had a farm just outside of Manistee. One time, he was selling old tools and farm stuff. I thought it would be cool to have this machete. I wanted to hang it on the basement wall, but that was a no go with Roseanne."

"I guess!"

"But now it's permanently under my bed. Hope that guy saw it and is too spooked to return."

"Me too, Dick. Believe me. Me too. You better get home and into bed."

"What are the chances I'll get back to sleep? Man, I wish I'd caught the guy."

"What can I say but thank you?"

"I know. I know. Just glad to be of help." He picked up the machete and was out the door. I now had my second wind. I poured a Pepsi and waited for Butch.

Just before Communion at the nine thirty Mass at Saint Joan of Arc that Sunday, I spotted a short, dark-haired man just five rows in front of me and to my left. On one side of him was a tiny elderly couple; on the other side was a couple with three fidgety teenage boys. Could this guy really be in our church? I thought that would be a stretch. Not hardly. But I kept staring at the back of his head, willing him to turn around.

Meanwhile, Butch was walking fussy Danny in the vestibule, Todd was lying under the pew in front of me, Seamus was trying to snap the hat/purse holder on the back of that pew, and Anne was on my lap rearranging the holy cards in my missal. Those behind us who understood smiled; those who didn't huffed.

Butch joined us as we filed out of the pew and headed to the altar for Communion. My eyes were trained on that man, and I held my breath. As he turned away from the priest and walked in front of the altar, I recognized him as a young son from one of the Greek families who lived on Hull Street. I exhaled and attempted to get into a prayerful state. Didn't work. In the car on the way home, I remembered when only my children had distracted me from my prayers.

Chapter Nine

A Trip to the Bar

The month of May was hot. Summer had arrived early. Heavy storm windows came down, and screens were scrubbed and put up. Windows were open, and the breeze blew the stale winter air out of the house. I relished the freshness, but nervousness hid around every corner of the season's joys. The main-floor windows were closed and locked nightly. I still lived under the delusion that this process would lock out my nightly fears as I trekked upstairs to begin my duty watch.

One night at about eleven, as I was reading a new best seller, the phone rang.

"Margo, it's Marv. Think I saw him. Take Chip in the bathroom and run the shower so he doesn't hear anything. Don't want him barking and scaring the guy." *Click.*

As the bathroom turned quickly into a sauna, I wondered when to come out. Chip stared at me quizzically and then laid his head on his paws, waiting, just as I was. Several minutes passed. Finally, I turned off the shower and peeked out of the bathroom, straining to hear a noise. Nothing. I led Chip down the stairs. He raced to the back door and just panted at the window. I looked out, and there was Marv, wearing a trench coat over his pajamas and loafers without socks, sporting a serious case of bedhead, and wielding a wooden baseball bat. Wide-eyed, I opened the back door.

"Marv, come on in. What happened? You OK? Did you see him?"

Marv obliged. He stood in the kitchen with his hands in his pockets, looking comical and very dejected.

"Dammit. I was checking the street before going to bed, and this guy was walking between the Trombleys two doors down and the Dolans. I figured I'd run to your backyard and clunk him with the bat when he came near your house. But when I got there, there was no one in sight. I checked all over. I don't get it."

"Maybe it wasn't the same guy. Maybe someone was just taking a shortcut. What'd he look like?"

"I dunno…shortish…dark clothes…no hat…dark hair. Crap."

"Look, Marv, you tried. He may have seen you and skedaddled. Something tells me that even if he wasn't the prowler, he would have skedaddled.Sorry. I guess I'm getting a little punch-drunk after all this."

He didn't smile, and I felt bad.

"You did your best, Marv, and Butch will be very grateful, just like I am. Get home. You know Marcia's waiting for the details."

This time he smiled and then headed for the door.

Despite the humorous happenings that night, vigilance became my armor everywhere I went, every minute of the day. I looked down each aisle and behind me at the grocery store. Once, as I was tossing boxes of Jell-O and pudding mixes into my cart, a swarthy man pushed his cart slowly by me. I was cemented to the floor. My hands tightly circled the cart handle, and I sucked in my breath. I could not look at his face as he passed by, but as he moved ahead, I saw that he was taller than my prowler, and, yes, his butt was flat. Another time in the hardware store's parking lot, I was leaning into the back seat giving animal crackers to the kids when the shadow of someone behind me blocked the sunlight. I whipped around and glared wide-eyed at an older man shuffling along toward the store. He didn't give me a second glance. At stoplights, I always looked to the right and left to see the drivers' faces. I was met with a half-smile, a nod, a bored stare, or a bothered toss of the head, but never the face I was seeking. Feeling frustration and relief at the same time confounded me.

My family and neighbors shared in my vigilance, looking for any signs of my tormenter's return. One Friday night around nine fifteen, my cousins Janet and Dori burst in my door, all excited and both jabbering at the same time.

"Hey, you two, bring it down. The kids are all asleep!"

They stood up straight and clapped their hands over their mouths.

"OK, one at a time. What's going on?"

"Margo, we saw your prowler!" Janet squealed.

"Yes, we saw him. We saw him!" Dori said. "We were stopped at a red light at the corner of Division and Burton, and there he was in a white dress shirt, black pants, that thick black hair you told us about, and a big nose. He was walking down Division Avenue and then went right into the Elbow Room. Get a babysitter. We'll check out the joint, and if he's still there, we can call the police and have him arrested. Hurry up. Hurry up!"

I called Barbara, Chris's oldest daughter. Since it was still light out, and if the guy really was at the bar, I figured he wouldn't be over here to threaten anyone. Luckily, Barbara was home and came right over.

We jumped into Janet's car and drove the fou- and-a-half blocks to the Elbow Room. Janet pulled into the gravel lot and

parked. Casually, we walked into the bar. My whole body became rigid at just the thought of seeing him. We strolled through,
glancing from table to table and searching the long bar, but
he was not there. Janet asked the bartender, "Did you happen
to see a short guy with dark pants and a dark jacket in here
tonight?"

"Yep. Earlier. He sat on that stool there." He pointed to one
right in front of us.

"Can you describe anything else about him at all?" I asked.

"This seems important to you ladies. And I guess there's
no harm in answering your question. He was very short, like
you said. Dark pants and a lightweight jacket."

"Anything else?" Janet asked.

"Well, I'm pretty good at details. His white shirt was neatly
ironed…maybe even starched. But what struck me the most
was his eyes, his stare. Eerie, if you know what I mean."

We all looked at one another, eyebrows raised.

The bartender continued. "He ordered a Coke and drank
half of it. Paid and over-tipped me and left. The guy was odd.
You ladies want a drink?"

"No, thanks," I said. "We have to get going. You were very
helpful. Thanks a lot, and have a good night."

He nodded and turned to wait on a couple who had just
arrived.

Once outside, Janet turned to us. "We should have come
here as soon as we saw him. We could have gone in or waited
until he came out."

"Yeah," Dori said. "And we could have followed him and
maybe found out where he lives. Why didn't we think?"

I said, "You weren't sure he was the guy. You really needed
me to be with you. I honestly don't know what I would have

done if I had seen him or if he had seen my face. But I'm telling you, that was him. That was definitely him."

We drove back to my house very slowly, the opposite of the way we had come, making a complete circle to look at every driveway, peering into every yard. But no luck. No sign of him at all. We were back at my house in half an hour.

Barb would not take any money for sitting. "My mom told me all about what's going on over here. At first I was creeped out and scared at my house. But then it was obvious you are the target. Why you, Mrs. Huver? You must have come in contact with him at some point. Don't you think? Or is this random? Just this morning after my nine o'clock western civ class, I was talking about all this with some friends. One girl's mom found a peeping tom at her window and screamed bloody murder. The guy ran off, and that was that."

"This is more than a peeping tom," I said. "This guy just seems to want to scare me, to keep me on edge. He's tried to get in at least once. I can't stop worrying about my kids. And I have no idea why he's after me, or what I can do to stop him. I wonder if I'll ever stop being afraid."

"Well, just call me anytime to watch the kids, Mrs. Huver. My class schedule this semester is pretty full, but I'm always home at night during the week."

"Thanks, Barb. That's good to know."

I watched her cross the street to her house. I would never have worried about her safety before. In fact, people around our neighborhood rarely even locked their doors when they were away, even for several hours.

I made a fresh pot of coffee, and we all sat in the dining room with our coffee, eating the brownies that I had baked earlier. As usual, we were discussing the impossible-to-catch prowler and just how he was disturbing everyone's lives. Such conversation made my insides shake. There was no controlling that.

Suddenly, a closet door in the kitchen slammed shut.

Dori screamed, "Oh, sweet Jesus! He's here! He's in the kitchen. Help us! Please help us! Dear God, please help us!"

Janet was jumping up and down in the middle of the room. "Help us! Anyone! Please help us!"

"Wait a minute!" I shouted at them. "Wait a minute."

The "intruder" appeared. There was Seamus's little angel face. His big blue eyes stared at me. I leaned over and picked him up, and, hugging him very tight, I whispered in his ear over and over, "I'm so sorry to scare you. I love you so much."

After everyone calmed down, I asked Seamus what had happened.

"I had a dream and woke up. I heard all the voices in the dining room and came downstairs and bumped into the kitchen closet, and it slammed shut, and then you guys were all screaming."

My sound sleepers seemed to be not so much lately. I ushered the little guy back to bed.

"Once again, we looked like Lucy, Ethel, and Fred," Janet said.

Dori whined, "I don't want to be Fred."

"Tough," Janet and I said.

We all laughed until Janet quietly ventured, "Man, Margo. How can you stand all this tension? Look how we went crazy."

I sighed and couldn't help the beginning of tears. "It's awful to live like this. Awful. Sometimes I think I'm losing my mind. But this sure proved, once again, that I do not want a gun. I can't even stand to think about it."

"Sweetie," Dori said, "please go up to bed and get some sleep. We'll wait for Butch to come home. Tomorrow's Saturday, and we don't have to get up early. Please?"

Tearfully I hugged them both, but I couldn't just go to bed.

Chapter Ten

A Minister, In-Laws, a Savior, and a Decision

Despite all of life's dramas, time was moving fast. It was the beginning of May, and our shop had been open one year. This was the last month of school for Seamus. Danny had been so much better since we'd added allergy shots to our practice of cleaning the bedroom. I was so relieved that no labored breathing was coming from his crib anymore. At the last appointment, the doctor told me, "If we can keep his sleep environment sterile for ten to fourteen hours a day, it will allow him to build up a resistance to his allergens to dust, mold spores, grasses, and the like. All your hard work is paying off, Mom." Hooray!

Yes, the prowler was still a thorn in my side, but I was allowing him to sting a little less. One afternoon, after a week in which all three of my protectors had been called but were not able to apprehend him, I allowed myself to think back on all the past incidents. I tried to remember them like a filmstrip and dispassionately examined each episode. His face had been in my window for several terrifying seconds. His presence had frightened me at the front door, the back door, the windows in the back of the house, and the windows on the sides of the house numerous times. Only Jimmy, the bartender, and I had ever seen his face. And wherever I went, I was always on edge, searching for him. Yet he had still not been caught. This guy was good; I gave him that.

The phone rang, breaking into my thoughts.

"Margo? Mom. Hi. Tomorrow I'll be tied up in real-estate meetings all day. Your little brothers have the day off. They haven't been over there in a while. Can I bring them for a sleepover tonight?"

"Sure, the kids will love that. I can pack lunches, and they can help me walk the kids to Garfield Park. I want to check on swimming lessons, and we can be back for Seamus to get to school."

"Perfect, honey. Thanks."

"Mom? How's Dad today?"

"Same. Guess that's good. Gotta go. Bye."

After dinner, Tim and Mark arrived, dragging their little black-and-white tweed suitcases. Soon, five kids chased and tumbled and somersaulted around the house. Danny tried to follow in his walker. Total chaos. Excedrin would be my friend tonight.

"All right, everyone, bedtime."

Todd whined, "Aww, Mom. We wanna stay up with Mark and Tim!"

Seamus added his pathetic, "Puleese?"

"OK. If you boys get in your pj's and brush your teeth, you can stay up a little longer. But no running around!"

They charged up the stairs, and I scooped up Anne and Danny and followed. By the time they were all asleep and I had cleaned up the kitchen and house, it was already ten thirty. I decided not to go up for duty watch, as Butch would be home in an hour and a half. Tim and Mark were sleeping soundly on the couch.

Feeling pretty brave, I raised the living-room windows a bit for some fresh air. I dozed on the chair and woke to "Here's Johnny!" Ten minutes into the monologue, I needed the bathroom. I decided to go upstairs and not disturb Chip. As I was washing my hands, *clang, clang, clang!* rang out from the backyard just below the bathroom window. All that was out there was a steel frame for a swing set. Charlie's kids had outgrown the set, and the swings had rusted out, so he had recently brought just the frame to us. We didn't have the time or the cash yet to purchase swings. No wind was blowing, and anyway, there was nothing on the steel frame that moved. But the banging continued. *Oh no. He's back.* I called Minister McGregor. He answered after one ring.

"God bless you, Margo. My in-laws are visiting from Indiana, and my father-in-law was getting ready for bed in the front guest room. He heard all the commotion coming from your house. We're on our way."

I ran back downstairs, turned off the television, and switched off the lights so the backyard would be easier to see. There was roly-poly Cornell and his father-in-law. Cornell was yelling at the top of his lungs.

"All right, you son of a bitch, we're going to kill you!"

Whoa! The minister? Swearing? And he was carrying a large rifle. The whole scene was a shock. This gentleman meant business. The two of them patrolled the neighborhood, repeating, "All right! You son of a bitch! We're going to kill you!" and aiming the rifle at everything in sight, under bushes, on front porches, behind garages. I met them on the front porch. Both of their faces were scarlet, and they were sucking air.

In a minute, Cornell said, "You know, dear, turning off the lights could have scared him away. Know what I mean?"

The father-in-law puffed in agreement.

"I guess you're right. But if that didn't scare him, you two sure did! Thank you," I said.

"Not a problem. Happy to help. Just call us if you need us," Cornell said.

The look from the father-in-law indicated he really hoped I wouldn't call. But as I stood on the porch, the two of them walked ramrod straight across the street.

The next morning, the kids and I were all out front, and old Shirley Cracco approached our house. Her light-blue flowered housedress flapped around her skinny calves. She wore a powder-blue, pop-bead necklace with two bracelets to match, and she padded up the driveway in blue slide-on slippers. The hint of blue in her white beehive finished off the vision.

"Dearie," she said, "I almost called the police last night when I saw two men charging around our block—and with a rifle, yet! I couldn't believe my eyes." She clutched her chest with both gnarly hands. "My heart isn't that strong, you know. Then I saw it was that Mr. McGregor. A man of God! Honestly, I didn't know what to think. And the older man with him was yelling to beat the band. Just what kind of commotion are you causing here?"

I took a few deep breaths before speaking. "Well, Shirley"—I knew she preferred Mrs. Cracco— "as you know, a prowler has been bothering me for a few months now, and the kind gentlemen around here are helping out since my husband is working nights."

"Can't you leave that to the police? They are certainly quieter about their business."

"The police have been called several times but haven't been able to help. Maybe you could sit by your front window tonight and watch for the guy, and then you could call the police?"

"Oh, no. I need my sleep, you know."

"Well, we just have to hope he doesn't come back then, don't we?"

"Yes. I just know this whole situation is too disturbing for me. I will have to sleep with my windows closed. Hope the heat won't affect my heart. Bye now."

I thought about offering her something to drink but just waved instead. Wagging her head, she shuffled back down the driveway.

Similar incidents with the prowler occurred during the last week of May, with the same lack of results. Each man was called at least once. Nothing. So frustrating. I was pretty convinced that the prowler was not out to physically hurt me, but the question of why persisted. I was worn down from constantly living under a thick cloud of "what next?" and the face in the window would not fade from my consciousness.

Then weeks went by, and no visits from the prowler. I hoped the appearances of my posse had scared him for good. That would be a miracle. I had accepted the axiom that into every life some rain must fall. But I was ready for this storm to cease.

By late August, new storm clouds were brewing, as Butch's mother, Vera, had now taken up residence in our dining room. On top of her myriad of life-threatening illnesses—uncontrollable brittle diabetes and severe heart problems as a result of childhood polio—she had announced that she was leaving Butch's father. He was "that mean old man," according to her. He had changed jobs very frequently, so they had to move several times during Butch's childhood. Butch had attended twelve different schools and never graduated.

Vera's doctor had instructed me to keep a record of how many heartbeats she had per minute and to count how many skipped beats. I was now a nurse. The two older boys seemed to understand that their grandma was pretty sick, and they gave her a wide berth around the dining room. Anne and Danny instinctively played around her bed. For several months, her days were definitely brightened. And I found myself enjoying adult conversation during dinner.

At this time, the shop was beginning to show modest profits. With Vera at the house, along with everything else, it was time to think about moving. On this subject, Butch was firm about one thing. "Once we buy another house and Seamus is in first grade, we will never move again. Our children will never be the 'new kid' after that."

I agreed.

One night in late November, the children were sound asleep, and the house was quiet as I checked Vera's heart rate. *Whoosh.* Chip came flying out of the back hall, knocking all the pans off the drain board in the kitchen. He growled, barked, and banged against the front door. Jumping up, I dropped Vera's skinny arm. I froze and made a clear decision not to look. Strung out, bone tired no energy…that was me.

Our house was now on the market, and Sundays after Mass were spent driving around neighborhoods near my folks while our realtor held an open house. Nothing in our price range was available, and we were discouraged.

Vera worsened, and after being hospitalized, she passed away in February of 1967. Losing his mother and facing what a sad life she had led was very difficult for Butch. We muscled through the aftermath of the funeral and continued to house hunt.

More rain entered our lives when Butch was moved to the graveyard shift at GM. His shift was from eleven p.m. to seven a.m., to begin in the middle of March. What was I going to do? I was still standing watch, but I couldn't stay awake all night. What if the prowler discovered that Butch was gone all those hours? Meanwhile, the shop continued to do a little better each month. We purchased supplies and grinding wheels, paid more on the overhead, and began a small nest egg, but it was not enough yet to support our family. I still wanted to move, and the sooner the better. But there were no offers on our house.

The first night of Butch's new shift came on the Ides of March, and I felt that doomsday was looming. At ten thirty, just before Butch was about to head to work, there was a *tap, tap, tap* on the front door. What in the world? Thank God, Butch was still home. He slowly opened the door, and there stood Barb Johansen, her khaki trench coat over a red plaid flannel nightgown that fell to the top of her pink bunny slippers.

Arms full with her knitting bag and textbooks, she announced, "My mom told me that Mr. Huver now has the graveyard shift. I'm here for the duration. I'll come over every night before Mr. Huver leaves and sleep on the couch till morning. I'll have plenty of time to go home and be ready for my classes." She continued, not letting us say a word. "I can't be comfortable across the street in my cozy bedroom knowing you're left alone with your little ones. I'm here. I'm staying. Get going, Mr. Huver, or you'll be late your first night."

"But the prowler hasn't been around in a couple of weeks," Butch said.

"I don't care," she said. "I just don't like the idea of Mrs. Huver being alone all night every night."

I gave her a hug. "Barb, you're a sweetheart and an angel. That Chris and Andy Johansen truly raised a wonderful daughter. Besides being in school, you're planning a wedding! We'll try this out and see how it works. The minute you need to go home, tell us."

"Promise?" Butch said.

"Sure. I promise."

That was the first night of over three weeks of nights that Barb stayed with me. What a joy it was to share wedding plans, house-hunting tales, and gossip from the block. Besides keeping a knife stashed between the mattress and box spring and my right arm out to grab it if needed, I was no longer obsessing about the prowler. On the night before her wedding, Barb sent her maid of honor to sleep on our couch. And the wedding was beautiful. Seamus, as the ring bearer, behaved and did a fine job, and Butch was proud to be a groomsman.

On a Friday night, Barb Johansen, now Barb Parker, walked into the Red Rocket Lounge with her new husband, Tom. The after-work crowd had sewn up all the tables, and "I Heard It through the Grapevine" pulsed from the jukebox. Luckily, two spots opened up at the bar. Snuggling shoulder to shoulder, the Parkers waited to order a beer and a burger. Rosemary Vander turned around, drying a pilsner glass.

"Hi there," she greeted the couple. Addressing Barbara, she said, "Say, I recognize you from our block on Lincoln. You live across the street from the Huvers, don't you?"

"I did. Not anymore. We've been married a month." Barbara held out her left hand. "This is my husband, Tom."

"Well. Congratulations. I know you're old enough to be married, but how about to drink?"

Barbara fished in her purse for her wallet and produced her driver's license.

"Just turned twenty-one last week."

"Congratulations again. What'll you both have?"

Tom answered, "Two Stroh's on tap and two cheeseburgers, two fries."

"Got it." Rosemary put in the order and returned to the couple. "Any news on that Mrs. Huver's prowler?"

"Nope," Barbara said. "I slept on her couch for a month when Mr. Huver went on midnights, and nothing. Maybe it's over."

"Sure hope so. You know, I saw a guy in my backyard the first night she called the police. Can't figure out why they don't help her. It's been months now. Oh, the bunch down there looks like they need more beer. Enjoy your burgers." Rosemary sidled down the bar, picking up dirty glasses and full ashtrays on the way.

Robby Ellison, out for fun with some buddies, was sitting next to Tom. He leaned forward to get Barb's attention.

"You know, I heard what you were talking about with the waitress just now. I'm on the force, and there's really nothing we can do when there's no corroboration or threat of violence." He decided not to let on that he was the one who had come to Margo's house that first night. "We have to be ready for more serious crimes and dangerous situations. Our department isn't that big. Not enough officers to go around, especially to trap prowlers. And, really, they're pretty harmless."

"Ooh, watch it, buddy," Tom said. "My wife is pretty protective of that lady and her little kids."

"Yeah. So what's she supposed to do when she's scared all the time?" asked Barbara.

"I dunno...just giving you how it is," Robby said, and he turned back to his buddies.

Rosemary appeared with their food. "Here you go. Hope you like everything."

They both nodded their thanks, and Tom turned to his wife. "It's pretty bad feeling so helpless, isn't it?"

"Imagine how she felt," Barb said.

Then they both picked up their hamburgers.

Shortly after the Parkers' wedding, I found that, yes, there was a God, as Butch was transferred back to afternoons. And the last time Chip bounded to the front door was as I was checking my mother-in-law's pulse. It was, I believe, the last appearance of my night visitor.

We had $1,500 now in our savings account, enough for a down payment on a new house. I scoured the classifieds every day for new listings of homes we could afford that had a dining room and, hopefully, a fireplace. Finally, a new ad was posted for a home just a mile from my mom and dad's. The next day, I enlisted Carol Ann to watch the children so I could check it out.

Oh, yes! I loved it! $12,000, and move-in perfect. It was a cute white Cape Cod with charcoal shutters and front door. Two bedrooms on the main floor and two bedrooms were up. There was a lot of open space with built-in white bookshelves and plenty of room for toys, but no fireplace and no family room. I spent the morning calling contractors inquiring about adding a family room with a fireplace. The best estimate was $3,000. This we could manage.

When Butch came home, I gave him all the details, especially the pertinent financial ones, and tried to keep my excitement down. The next day would be June 3, his birthday.

"Honey, this is perfect. With you taking your birthday off tomorrow, we can look at the house before the family comes for cake and ice cream."

"Sounds good. Make an appointment, Margo."

"I already did."

"No surprise there. You are something else."

"I know...and usually right too." We toasted with our coffee mugs.

Butch totally approved the new house. I knew he would. Sitting in the car out front, Butch said, "You know, Margo, liking this new house is just part of it. I want off of Lincoln Street, away from the prowler, away from you living in fear each night, away from me having the same fear and not able to protect you and the kids—the whole thing."

"I know. I know." I sighed. "Me too. Now we have to call the owners and make an offer before someone else does. Offer full price. Whatever it takes—I mean it."

"Hold your horses, there. Offer full price? No way. That's not how business is done."

"But honey..."

"But honey, nothing. Let me handle this."

I knew now was the time to be quiet.

Driving away, I took in the particulars of the neighborhood: bungalows, ranches, two-story colonials, and a few more Cape Cods—a nice variety of homes. Tall maple trees lined both sides of the wide street. I peeked into some backyards and was pleased to see swing sets and sandboxes—barometers for a neighborhood for families with small children.

That evening after the family left, the two little ones were already asleep, and Seamus and Todd were playing Monopoly. I had been researching homes, prices, and the market for several months, and I knew the value of this house. I didn't want to lose it. Taking a deep breath, I dialed the number and handed the phone to Butch. He spoke calmly and softly. Me? I was jumping up and down, circling my hand for him to get to the point. Finally, they were discussing price. My eyes held Butch's with a stare that said, "Do not lose this house." The seller agreed to a land contract, and we would close in two weeks, not later than June 21. Yahoo!

Selling our own home was more complicated. In fact, it did not sell, so we eventually decided to rent it. Construction had begun on the improvements to our new home, and the kids and I tried to go over every night after dinner to check on the progress. On the evening of July 25, my mom said to leave the kids with her and to take my dad over. Great idea! He brought a flashlight so he could inspect every inch. Of course, he discovered water in the hole prepared for the new fireplace that was to be installed the next day, and he insisted we bail, and we did, pail by pail.

By the time we returned to my parents' home, it was ten forty five in the evening, way past everyone's bedtime. As I gathered up the toys, the phone rang. It was my brother, John.

"Margo! Do not go home by your regular route. Go way around to Burton and come back to your house. Do not take the cemetery shortcut!"

"What's the matter? Why not?"

"I was driving down Division and stopped at a red light. All of a sudden, the street was filled with black boys yelling and screaming, a real mob scene. My windows were down, and one of the guys punched me in the face. I was bleeding."

"What? Are you all right?"

"Yes. Yes. I stopped by your house to clean up while no one was there. Don't tell Mom. She'll just worry until I get home."

"OK, John. I'll tell her you were warning me about a street being closed."

I piled the kids into the car, and they were asleep in minutes. I didn't run into any trouble on the way back, and they were soon tucked into their beds without even waking up. Butch came home, and after his light supper, we went off to bed.

In the middle of the night, the phone rang. That was always frightening! *Someone must be sick or dying.* My mind couldn't help jumping to shades of my mother's alarmist temperament. I stretched across Butch to answer the phone.

My cousin Janet was screaming hysterically, "Margo, are you sleeping? Get up! The city's on fire!"

"Oh, go on." I glanced at the clock. It was one fifteen. I had only been asleep for about twenty minutes. "What are you talking about?"

"Get up! Look out your bathroom window. Go!"

I put the phone down, went into the bathroom, and pulled back the curtains. Now I yelled, "Oh my God! Oh my God! The city *is* on fire! Butch, wake up!" I ran back and picked up the phone. "Thank you, thank you, Janet! I'm leaving this house and never staying here another night! The prowler and now this. Good-bye!"

"Get moving!" Janet shouted.

I quickly called my mom and told her the riots had started here and that our family was coming over now.

"Of course. I'll put the porch light on. Hurry," she said.

By now, Butch knew what was going on. We loaded the car with essentials. Luckily, the laundry was finished and folded but not put away; the baskets were added to the car. I grabbed a Pepsi as I flew around the kitchen, packing refrigerator items. Next were vitamins, allergy meds, baby food, and some toys. Butch woke the kids, trying not to scare Seamus and Todd and prodding them down the stairs as he carried Anne and Danny. Everyone was in the car when I ran back into the house to grab the mail. I glanced around, taking in that we didn't live here anymore.

Butch backed down the driveway and headed toward Division. As we drove to the bottom of the hill, officers with raised rifles surrounded their squad cars. So frightening! The street was blocked, and an officer approached our car.

"The riots have started here. Go south to Burton and then east only. Please be careful." Butch rolled down the widow and asked him, "What's going on?"

"Too much unrest, I guess. Don't know what sparked the whole thing, though. Just trying to protect all the citizens. You better get going, sir."

Butch nodded and rolled the window back up, and we drove away.

My mom, dad, sister, and brothers welcomed all six of us into their home, knowing full well how crowded and chaotic life would be. Luckily, it would be only ten days before all the new house renovations were complete. By August 1967, we were happily settled into our new home, Seamus was enrolled in school, and I was free of fear.

Chapter Eleven

June 1968, The Face in My Window

We had been living in our new home for almost a year—hard to believe. I was so happy with the house, and we had great next-door neighbors. Seamus loved Saint Thomas, and Todd was thriving in kindergarten at Michigan Oak. Anne and Danny played together well now; he went along with whatever she dreamed up.

The shop was thriving. We figured Butch would have to work about two-and-a-half more years at GM. I loved to imagine our future life. Our new environment allowed me to be more relaxed, but I could not totally let my guard down. The butcher knife remained tucked under my mattress, and I automatically scanned people at the mall or wherever I was throughout town. I hoped upon hope the prowler would be caught, at the same time knowing that the chances of this were less than slim.

At the end of May, once again, Butch was put on the six p.m. to six a.m. shift at GM. On Tuesday, June 4, he left for work as usual, expecting a full shift. Around three in the morning, a power outage closed down the factory, and the entire workforce was told to leave. On his way home, a news alert blasted from the van radio: "Senator Robert

Kennedy has been shot while leaving the Ambassador Hotel in Los Angeles after making his acceptance speech for the California presidential primary."

I awoke to Butch gently tapping my shoulder. "Margo, honey. Wake up. Bobby Kennedy has been shot, and that's all I know. I'll make a pot of coffee and turn the television on."

"What?" I blinked and then rubbed my eyes, trying to grasp what he had just told me. Then I shouted, "No! No!" I think I loved and respected Bobby more than his brother. "This can't be happening again." I grabbed my robe, tightening the belt as I ran into the family room. The broadcast was on live from California, and now we felt he was close to death. Butch brought in the coffee mugs, and I stared at the swirling steam.

"That poor family!" I cried. "And our poor country. JFK and then Dr. King a few months ago! What's going on?" I curled into Butch's arm. A steady stream of tears slipped down my face. My instinct was to call my family, but it was the middle of the night. We witnessed the confusion in the hotel kitchen for at least a half-an-hour. Butch slipped his arm off my shoulder, placed his cup on the end table, and stretched out on the couch, falling asleep.

Concentrating was difficult for me because scads of reporters were talking at the same time. I leaned in to try to catch all the details. The consensus was that the shooter didn't have any identification on him but had four hundred dollars in his pocket. They were looking for some girl in a polka-dot dress. A camera suddenly swung dizzily around and focused on the face of the shooter. I fell to my knees from the couch, my coffee now a puddle sinking into the carpet. I stood up and started screaming. Butch woke up and stumbled up next to me. "What? What's the matter?"

"Oh my God! Oh my God! No! No! It's him! It's him! The face in the window!"

"What?"

"It's him—the prowler—the face in my window. I could never forget it. Never. As long as I live."

"How can that be? How do you know it's him?"

"Because I saw his face for all those seconds. That image has never left me. I'm telling you; it's him."

My knees buckled as I walked to the kitchen to get a rag. As I blotted the coffee from the rug, my whole being seemed to be whirling. Utter sadness at this wonderful man's death was coupled with giant relief. My prowler had been caught and would never bother me again. I sat back against the couch. It was as if a million butterflies were taking all the fears and tensions out of my body up and away forever. Still stunned, I turned to Butch, but he was back asleep. I resisted the urge to call my mom, my sisters, everybody. They were all still asleep and oblivious to this tragedy.

Covering myself with the ecru mohair afghan my mom had knitted for us as a housewarming gift, I put my head back and drifted into a twilight sleep. My eyes popped open a few hours later, and I let the happenings of the night sink in. I slowly rose from the couch and walked silently into the kitchen. I picked up the phone and called everyone in turn: "Mom?"

"Joni?"

"Janet?"

"Dori?"

"Carol Ann?"

"Geraldine?"

"Chris?"

"Marcia?"

Our conversations were filled with what-ifs. "What if the police had taken me more seriously? What if fingerprints could have been evidence? What if one of my knights on Lincoln had caught him? Would any of that have delayed Sirhan from getting to California? Would it have scared him away from his horrible plan?"

Snippets of our conversations that morning went like this:

Mom: "Oh, honey, I'm so relieved that you're finally really safe! But Dad and I are just so sad that such a wonderful man was gunned down. We just can't make sense of any of it."

Joni: "No more worrying about you and your family, Margo. No more worrying. Oh! My prayers for you have been answered. But the poor family...all those children, and Ethel being pregnant..."

Janet: "Why couldn't we have caught him in that bar? I could have gone in and stalled him or something while Dori got you. He could have been stopped from all this horror!"

Dori: "Kiddo, kiddo. I think we did all we could. But so sad, so sad. Just have to keep thanking God you and Butch and the kids are OK."

Carol Ann: "I am glued to the television even though I can't stop crying. So scared when I think of what he could have done to you. A madman!"

Marcia: "We were all frightened for you. But—but he's a killer! A cold-blooded killer."

Chris: "So, do you think the police will listen to you now?"

Janet: "The FBI?"

Marcia: "The CIA?"

In the days and weeks following the assassination, I was fixated on the television set, absorbing information from every newscast and closely reading every page of the *Grand Rapids*

Chronicle. There were never any photos of Sirhan from behind. But I didn't need them. He was my prowler.

And, like the wounded nation, I watched and cried as Andy Williams sang "The Battle Hymn of the Republic" during the heart-wrenching funeral at the stately and beautiful Saint Patrick's Cathedral in New York City. Then we all witnessed the nonstop train traveling over thousands of coins placed on the tracks as it carried Senator Kennedy's body from the cathedral over two hundred miles to Arlington National Cemetery. The now lone Kennedy brother, Ted, waved from the caboose to the unbroken line of mourners in each city and town along the route. People were on platforms, in trees, in the fields, on apartment balconies, on the roofs of buildings. Signs like WE LOVE YOU, BOBBY and GOOD-BYE BOBBY punctuated the grief.

Awash in my emotions, I was constantly aware that the assassin had confronted me too. I loathed him for all he was to me, to the Kennedy family, and to our country. Sirhan was no longer a threat to me physically, but the memory of his persona never left me. Butch and I had several conversations concerning whether or not I should come forth and to whom. At first, thinking about this panicked me; I wasn't sure why. But the more I read and the more I listened to national news, the more I was able to understand my serious unease.

The year President John Kennedy was assassinated; I was a twenty-two-year-old with two babies. I accepted the Warren Report—that Lee Harvey Oswald had been the lone gunman. Like most of our country, that was what I wanted to believe, and I left it at that. This time, in my own isolated way, I had been personally involved, so I absorbed all reports of possible conspiracies and motives—from those of the esteemed television journalist Walter Cronkite to those of venerable newspapers and even crackpot pundits. My discovery was that Robert Kennedy's enemies had been numerous and some extremely powerful. For a few, their hatred ran deep.

As US attorney general, Kennedy had ruthlessly gone after corruption in the teamsters' labor union. His investigations resulted in his belief that the union's president, Jimmy Hoffa, had extorted, worked with mobsters, and stolen from the teamsters pension funds. Hoffa had spent time in prison due to Kennedy's campaign against him. He had been quoted as saying, "I've got to do something about that son of a bitch Bobby Kennedy. He doesn't have any guards on his house. What do you know about plastic bombs?" Hoffa subsequently disappeared, but his body has never been found, of course. Old mysteries kept surfacing for me. I also uncovered a rumor that I could not verify that Sirhan Sirhan continued to receive money while in prison; it supposedly was traced to the teamsters' union. Sifting fact from fiction was challenging and contributed to my desire to keep pushing for the truth.

Most Americans were aware that FBI Director J. Edgar Hoover was always at odds with Robert Kennedy because he felt Kennedy had too much power. One of his deputies at a meeting of senior FBI agents once said, "I hope someone shoots and kills that son of a bitch."

I hadn't followed too much of the Mafia's problems with Robert Kennedy. But after the assassination, I tuned in to how during his term, convictions against organized crime members had risen by 800 percent. One don, Carlos Marcello, had been deported to Guatemala for several years. He had endured being kept in a Central American jungle by the local military and at one point was lost in a rain forest for three days. He still had tremendous influence and at the time of the killing was back in the United States. The idea or reality of the mob involved somehow with Sirhan gave me pause, to say the least.

I had loved Robert Kennedy for his brashness and willingness to pull for all Americans. I was young, busy, and not really involved in politics, but all his speeches tugged at my emotions. Even though he had been unbelievably privileged, he cared about those living in poverty. He worked to improve the lives of Native Americans in substandard living conditions. The failure of America's great wealth to reach so many of its citizens dismayed him.

And I respected Senator Kennedy so much for his work for civil rights. So many black people had supported and admired him. Several articles appeared in the *Grand Rapids Chronicle* on June 6. One was titled "Many See Racial Overtones in Kennedy Slaying." A Harlem housewife said, "Every time a colored or a white fellow tries to help us make a better life for ourselves, somebody will cut him down for no reason." I remembered Senator Kennedy saying in an interview a few years before that crime wasn't the biggest American problem...civil rights for all was. The segregationists, the racists, all hated him, as far as I could see.

Big business resented him for involving the FBI in looking at price fixing. The list of enemies I found went on and on. And, just like in the assassination of President John Kennedy, hints arose about the CIA being involved. I never figured out why then, but just the mention of the CIA scared me.

The paranoia—deservedly, I felt—that dogged me in 1966 loomed much larger for me in 1968. So, should I go to the police? No. My contacts with the Grand Rapids Police Department in 1966 had gone nowhere. Even if my complaints had been followed up on, I couldn't imagine the department admitting that it could inadvertently have been partly responsible for this senseless death. And Butch and I did not want our names blacklisted with the police going forward. What about the FBI? The CIA? No. No way. I still feared for my safety and, more importantly, that of my family. I continued to search for any new details about the assassination and to pore over the newspaper clippings I had saved. I had diligently kept notes and knew that someday they would be important. I just knew it.

On June 4, at the change of shifts, the officers were gathering in the squad room. Sergeant Grubowski leaned on a wooden lectern in the front of the sparse room. DeVos and Majewski were the last to arrive, finding two empty metal folding chairs on the side of the room.

"What's up, Sarge?" Officer Ellison asked.

"Robby, we've gone through the race riots and the aftermath of the killing of Martin Luther King. Everyone listen up. Go over our procedures and our new tactics with your partners. Tensions are still running high from those events. I don't want any repeats of violence or any citizens getting hurt. You all know what to do. And no stopping for coffee or doughnuts or to shoot the shit with another cruiser. Stay alert. Be ready to defuse. Man, I just can't get over another Kennedy being killed." His head dropped down. "OK. Be careful out there."

Part II

Chapter Twelve

Time Flies

Where does the time go? How could so much transpire in what seems to be a blink of an eye? As I was reflecting on my life, I felt as if I was at a crossroad. Life's challenges had been met, many heartbreaking, many heartwarming, and some monumental. Our children were raised and educated and had begun families of their own. Ten adorable and delightful grandchildren were born, and now one great-granddaughter had joined our family.

Of our many traditions, heading to Pentwater the Friday before Father's Day was one that topped my list. I had to laugh; I never thought I would like camping. Our first adventure started back in 1969. Our neighbors insisted we take their pop-up camper. I LOVED IT. This was the first time I told my story around a campfire in Pentwater, Michigan on the shores of Lake Michigan.

On the same day every year, the Friday before Father's Day, we would head to Pentwater. The six of us would crowd into that pop-up camper. We would add a tent for the kids to bring friends. As the years passed we later graduated to a motor home. By this time, seven other families and their extended families would join us. Our campsites took over the north end of the campground. We had a couple large, screened enclosures where the cooking and picnic tables were stationed. The fire pit at the base of Old Baldy trail was the designated campfire pit. The men pitched in and cooked breakfast for everyone, and the kids did the dishes. The rest of the day was spent swimming, hiking, tossing footballs and Frisbees, reading, cribbage tournaments, and sunbathing. It seemed that there was always a child or two whittling away on the perfect stick for cooking hot dogs or marshmallows.

At night, the grown-ups played euchre or poker, and the children circled their beach chairs and blankets around the campfire, roasting marshmallows and cooking s'mores. One of the children would always come get me and drag me to the campfire so I could tell them my stories. I began with their favorite one by staring into the fire and following the red-gold sparks and the gray smoke up into the night air. Then, looking around at all their expectant, glowing faces, I would tell my story. And as the years went by, their children, and then their children's children, heard the same tale.

It's hard to believe that over 40 years later I still head to our favorite spot to be with family and friends.

Over the years each of the kids had at one time or another worked with Butch at the shop. It was a family affair. As our kids got older, life took them in different directions. Before long each had finished their schooling, worked at *the shop* and other places, met their future spouses, got married, and then had children and homes of their own.

This seemed like a good time for me to start a career of my own. With this change, Seamus eventually took over my job of running the office for *the shop*. I became a Realtor. I was having so much fun and soon became top seller month after month. I wanted to offer more to my clients so I became a real-estate broker. Eventually I found a partner to start a real-estate agency of my own.

Butch was ready to pass down his business. At the time Dan was the one still working at the shop and seemed the most logical choice. Seamus was taking care of the office and books while traveling to handle the financials of a radio station. Butch took a huge leap of faith and began the purchase of a rundown restaurant, bar, and sports complex. This venture became quite a struggle with countless obstacles to overcome.

I wanted to help Butch, but how? I knew if I was going to be of any help I would need to end this career that I truly loved.

I worked as the kitchen manager, wedding planner, entertainment coordinator, and personnel manager. This place consumed us as we took it from a failing, falling apart restaurant/bar sports complex to a stable family restaurant/event venue, The Westwood. Not my dream job but that's what you do for the love of your family.

Throughout the years, I had heard, "Mom," or "Grandma," or "Margo, you should put your amazing story down. Write a book. We loved hearing it, and what you have to say is important."

Several times, I sat down to do so but could not get started and told myself that I didn't have the time anyway. The latter was certainly true, but I also was consumed with self-doubt. I hadn't gone to college. But I had taken specific notes those weeks after the assassination, and I had retold what happened in detail so many times. All was still very clear in my head. Orally, I was confident, but I just couldn't write it down. I didn't know how to begin on paper. I couldn't even decide what tense to write it in. At the time, this challenge was a cinder-block wall. No ladder. No rope.-No book. - Life continued on.

For fifteen years we worked together until the shocking discovery of Butch's cancer. I remember it like it was yesterday when the doctor called me and the kids into a conference room to go over the pathology report - stage-four metastatic melanoma. My world was still reeling from news that Butch needed urgent brain surgery to remove one of the two tumors. How could this be? We just celebrated our 50th wedding anniversary. He was working the day he was admitted to the hospital. The reality of it never really set in. While our world continued spinning all around us, I never left his side. December 28th, 2009 was the day we received the news we should begin hospice for Butch. On that same day my younger brother, Tim, unexpectedly passed away. Butch's health had taken a sharp turn and he wasn't able to attend Tim's funeral on January 2nd. I had scheduled for the hospice nurse to come the next day. She confirmed that there was no time to waste. Within three days of getting his hospital bed set up in the living room he was gone. How could that be? And fifteen quick weeks his life was taken.

What a way to start this New Year, 2010 rang in with a bang. I didn't have to close my eyes and I didn't need a photo album or technology to remember our fifty years of life together. It's as if I had an internal View-Master, one like those our children played with when they were young. I can click through and see Butch with his James Dean twinkle, his steadfastness in building a business, and his pride as each of our children reached milestones. I can see him struggling with his traditional attitudes, such as when Anne was beginning to look at colleges.

Butch felt that Anne would be just as well-off sticking close to home and settling down.

I can see us dancing through the years at special events and just because we loved it. Our traveling and special trips click by. The absolute worst part of a loving and successful marriage is that one person has to go first, leaving his or her spouse alone to negotiate the rest of life. Like so many others, I struggled and survived the grieving process and came out on the other side, making a list of affirmations punctuated by items from the now-popular bucket list: honor Butch's last request to clean out the basement, travel, play bridge, seek out more quality time with the grandchildren, maybe have a boring day or two, and, yes, write a book. Life wouldn't let me get to my list just yet.

From the day of Butch's surgery, Seamus was left on his own to run The Westwood. He never complained. He never said he wouldn't or couldn't do it. He just handled it...much like his father would have. Except this time I knew I could not come back and help him.

I had about all I could handle with trying to tie up all the loose ends after Butch's death. I didn't want to face clearing out the house where Tim had lived. What choice did I have, he was living in our duplex. There was no way I wanted to be a landlord on my own. I had to get it ready to put up for sale. Once that was done, I put much of my focus on clearing out the basement, replacing the furnace, water heater, repairing the roof and the leak in the living room. I was shocked how neglected our home had become. I finally felt as if I was reaching my new normal... I just can't believe it. NO. Why?!

Anne's voice was so distant, so frail, and so sad. I thought I heard her wrong. I had to say –"What?" I didn't want to make her repeat herself; I just couldn't believe what I was hearing. "Oh honey, I am so sorry. How I wished I were there." I wanted to hug her and let her know she could count on me. Anne's husband, Steve, was diagnosed with stage-four small-cell lung cancer that had metastasized to his liver and lymph glands. Anne, Steve, and their fourteen-year-old daughter, Paige, lived in the suburbs of Chicago. Even though Glen Ellyn was only three hours away, this chasm caused such sadness it might as well have been a thousand miles away, because I couldn't just stop over to give them hugs or bring dinner. I made numerous trips but couldn't be the help I wanted to be. Anne was barely finished grieving for her dad, and now she faced this dreadful disease all over again with her young husband and only daughter. A wonderful husband, father, and son-in-law. Steve was also a faithful employee and worked right up to the last two weeks of his life. He passed away on August 10, 2013.

I had brought up selling The Westwood numerous times to Seamus. He didn't want to do this to his staff. I knew that I needed to be the one who made the decision. After a long talk with Seamus he finally agreed. We decided to close the complex on August 15, 2013, and that chapter of my life was now coming to an end.

Chapter Thirteen

Kismet

On November 19, 2013, we met with the future buyers of the sports complex to sign the purchase agreement. All the papers were signed, and the buyers left the complex. Wow! I could feel the weight and worry of the past lighten...a new life in front of me. I knew there was still a lot of work ahead for me. I would have to find a way to clear out this huge facility before the closing. However, there was no time to breathe, because my packed suitcase was in the trunk. Seamus and I were off for the three-hour drive to Chicago. We were joining Anne and Paige flying to Pittsburgh for a ceremony honoring Steve. I was prepared for the event to be emotional, and I knew my job was to be support for Anne, who had taped a message for the gathering. She didn't trust herself to speak. Steve's whole family and part of mine would be joining us.

One of Steve's company's suppliers was dedicating a new training facility in their building to Steve. His penchant for fairness and his special talents had helped tremendously in bringing the supplier expansion and success. A charming guest house at a posh old country club was rented for all thirteen of us. We were treated to dinner, breakfast, lunch, a tour of the facility, and the very moving dedication. Throughout our days in Pittsburgh, I marveled at this unique experience of a major company honoring a contributor and collaborator such as Steve, who was not even an employee.

At breakfast that morning, I was seated next to Janet, the wife of the man responsible for organizing the dedication. She was a retired educator who had taught literature and creative writing and had published two educational books. She presently volunteered at a student-mentoring organization in Chicago and lived not far from Anne. We chatted amicably and seemed to connect. Later, all of us attended a lunch in a contemporary restaurant. The floor-to-ceiling windows afforded a view of a snow scape of white shapes over shrubs and bushes and trees. I found myself seated next to the same woman from breakfast. I also found myself telling her that it was time for me to write a book. I shared the premise that in 1966, twenty-five years old and the mother of four children under five, I had been stalked in Grand Rapids by a famous man.

Janet asked, "Famous? In Michigan? 1966? Was it Governor George Romney? President Gerald Ford? Don't think so! Who could it possibly be?"

"No, no." I laughed. "I should have said 'infamous.'"

"Give me a description."

"Short. Dark skin. Dark hair. Dark eyes."

After a minute, she whipped around to face me. "Not Sirhan Sirhan?"

How had she come up with that? When I said yes, she let out a squeal, as did other guests around the table who were listening to our conversation. Family members across the dining room smiled and nodded at us, knowing I was once again sharing my experience.

"The problem is," I told her, "I have this great story, but even though I've tried on and off, I just can't put it on paper."

"Here's your solution," Janet said. "I don't have a story. But I can write." Right then and there, we shook hands on our partnership. Excitedly, she said we could travel to the California prison and interview Sirhan. Transported back forty-seven years, my body shook. To be in the same room as my tormentor, that killer of Bobby Kennedy? No way. That subject was closed.

Before the luncheon was over, we settled on our strategy. I would speak into a special computer program, recalling each incident, and e-mail the files to her. She would write a chapter and then return it to me, and we would go over it together on the phone. Was this meeting kismet? Karma? The Holy Spirit? Whatever name one chose for it, I knew Steve had made sure to help me from above. Even though I was uneasy and a bit frightened as I revisited all those episodes, I knew the timing was perfect to tell my story and perhaps solve the mystery of why.

Part III

Chapter Fourteen

The Beginning of the Thread

In June 1968, after the shock of recognizing my stalker, wildly imagining how Senator Kennedy's killing might have been avoided, and experiencing waves of perhaps irrational paralyzing fear, I was compelled to try to make sense of everything. After clipping every single newspaper article I could, I took pages of notes of pertinent information, television broadcasts, and any theory I could think of linking Sirhan to Grand Rapids and to me. This time, my anxiety was not about fear for my safety or that of my family but fear of what disclosing this information would mean.

Forty-six years had passed since the assassination of Robert Kennedy. Each day back then, I had read everything I could about it. Since then, a myriad of books, newspaper and magazine articles, websites, and so on had examined the assassination. I was astounded at all the information that was new to me. For instance, many sources agreed that there was no way that Sirhan Sirhan acted alone. Sirhan's gun held eight bullets, but thirteen bullets were fired, only four at the senator. Five others were also shot at the time. Bullets were found in a door molding and a ceiling tile. The two bullets that killed Kennedy came at close range from behind, while Sirhan had been several feet in front of the senator.

Three days before the killing, it was said that a Los Angeles police officer took Sirhan to a shooting range and spent hours with him, using expensive ammunition. Sirhan had no money. Sirhan was seen with a young woman the day before the shooting. Also that day, he and some young man were hitchhiking and picked up by a man who later went to the police. He told the police that another time he had gone to the Ambassador Hotel to collect money for a horse he was to get for Sirhan. At the hotel, this man witnessed Sirhan with a girl and three other men. The man's account was not taken seriously because he had a criminal record. But why would he make up seeing those people?

Many accounts of a possible second gunman, a security guard, have been detailed. My head spun after reading pages about this guy, his behavior, his testimonies. What I understood was that this man was employed as a maintenance plumber at an aircraft plant and had security clearance from the Department of Defense. He had moonlighted for a guard service and had been hired to protect Kennedy at the Ambassador Hotel that night. Directly behind the senator in the kitchen, he said he pulled a gun after the first shots rang out but did not get an opportunity to fire, as he was pushed back by Kennedy when the senator fell.

The LAPD had interviewed the security guard but did not ask to see his gun. This guard was interviewed several times at intervals, and his story always seemed to change. One important fact was that this guard said he had previously sold a gun like the one that killed Kennedy. After checking with the buyer and seeing the signed receipt, an LA policeman found that the pistol had actually been sold three months *after* the assassination. Years later, this security guard submitted to a reputable lie detector examination and denied any involvement in the murder. He passed the test. So, did the two shots from behind that killed Kennedy come from this guy's gun? This was never determined. I later learned that the man had hated both JFK and RFK and was an admitted racist. I knew, unfortunately, that this information did not prove anything.

Several individuals had witnessed a girl in a polka-dot dress running from the kitchen entrance of the Ambassador Hotel screaming, "We've killed him!" All accounts, for one reason or another, were deemed phony or false.

The FBI confiscated a camera and three rolls of film with thirty-six photos on each belonging to a high-school student who had taken photos for his school newspaper. After Kennedy's acceptance speech, the young man followed the senator into the pantry and was standing on a table shooting pictures when the shots were fired. He continued clicking with his arm raised to capture what was happening although he could not see it himself because of all the confusion. The police, a medical team, and Ethel arrived. The young man left to find his friend. On exiting the Ambassador Hotel, he was tackled by the FBI, and his camera and film were confiscated. He was removed to a room in the hotel and questioned until four a.m. The police then escorted him to their headquarters, where he was questioned further and was finally allowed to leave at six a.m. He was told his camera and film would be returned after the trial. This all made sense, but all that was given to him were glossies of the senator giving his speech.

Years later as an adult, the student sued for the return of his property. However, the agent returning the photos and equipment to the man was carjacked and his briefcase stolen. The photographer never received his film or camera.

What about Sirhan's connection to me? In 2014, I was armed with the artifacts rescued from the back of the linen closet. How many times had I moved that box around as I reorganized the closet? Each time, I thought about writing all this down and really attempting to begin my book. Finally, I was ready. This time, my heart was fluttering with anticipation for what I might discover and the possibility that my story would really be out there beyond my intimate world.

I thoroughly researched the killing of Bobby Kennedy, settling on two legitimate sources as well as several secondary sources on the Internet. I needed to dig and sift through all of it to find a connection to me. That connection, that thread, began with articles in the *Grand Rapids Chronicle* from June 9, 1968. Upon first reading this years ago, I had wondered if the subjects of two articles in the paper were one and the same. Throughout the years, I often contemplated this possibility. Now it was time to really check it out.

Fueled by adrenaline, I opened a yellowed newspaper to pages three and four and spread it out on my kitchen counter. There they were. Two articles had appeared in the same edition of the paper. On the left page, the article "Polka-Dot Girl Was Wrong One" dealt with a key witness seeing a girl in a polka-dot dress fleeing from the hotel minutes after the assassination. On the right side of the page was an article headlined "Girl Left Without Cause; Left College to Help RFK." A staffer reported an interview with this college student, Elaine Peters, from WRC, White Rapids College, in Grand Rapids. This girl dropped out of college midterm and joined RFK's campaign staff. She was in California the night of the shooting. I suppose because she attended a local college and was a volunteer for the RFK campaign headquarters, the reporter had sought her out for this interview.

What really intrigued me was her behavior after the shooting. She did not attend the funeral, and she did not ride the train with the body to Arlington National Cemetery. If she had interrupted her college career for the senator and worked for months on the campaign, why didn't she take part in the end of Robert Kennedy's story? And why didn't she go home to her family after experiencing this tragedy? Or to her boyfriend in Indiana? Instead, she left California and returned to Grand Rapids—where she was *not* taking classes—to see a college professor. What a surprise, that professor just happened to live a few blocks from our home on Lincoln. The thread had turned a tiny bit toward me.

When the young coed joined Kennedy's campaign, she was trained in Grand Rapids, then sent to Mackinac City, Michigan, to help the workers. Later, she was reassigned to travel to the organization's headquarters in Los Angeles to be there ready for work on May 18. I had seen pages from one of Sirhan's journals in one of the old newspapers. One page had "May 18" written over and over. A connection.

I needed to get to the library to see if I could find more information from that time period. Our Michigan winter of 2014 was more than brutal. This area had always been the snow capital of the Midwest, but the days were typically sunny, the roads plowed efficiently, and we hearty Michiganders went about our lives without letting weather hamper us. But this winter had hit us with a record number of days hovering around or below zero. Several feet of snow formed a white quilt over everything, and that quilt kept getting deeper. Plows just could not keep up. The neighbor boy I had contracted to shovel my long double driveway showed up one morning after an additional two and a half feet of the white stuff had fallen during the night. His shoulders were slumped, and I swear he was practically in tears. I doubled his tip that day.

That morning was two degrees with fifteen-mile-an-hour winds. I dressed for downhill skiing. Our street was nothing but two ruts, but I determinedly braved the trail to downtown. By the time I stepped out of the car in the east parking lot of the main branch of the Grand Rapids Public Library, snow was falling again—well, not falling, but blowing horizontally. I pinched my fur-lined hood closer around my face, but the snow needles still found my nose and forehead.

The library building was typical of turn-of-the-century design, showing a strong civil architecture. The exterior walls were of large, gray rectangular stones, and the heavy, ornately carved cornice seemed incongruous on the functional walls. I trudged up the twenty-five steps to the library. In the spacious vestibule, a few patrons and I stomped the snow from our boots and peeled off some of the layers of our clothing.

A creaky and shaky elevator with teakwood walls and a hammered copper ceiling took me to the fourth floor, which was devoted to the city of Grand Rapids only. I deposited my damp white puffy jacket, black North Face gloves, and imitation Burberry scarf on a chair. My "briefcase," a Meijer shopping bag containing a folder of articles, my purse, a notebook and pens, and two books on the assassination, was slung over my shoulder as I searched for the microfiche station. My, my. Back in the day, they used to have those little cans with tiny rolls of film that were threaded into a small machine. We had to press our eyes against a viewer and manually roll the film to find our information. Here were screens the actual size of a newspaper page. A gizmo like a mouse was used to move from page to page. Very cool.

I sat down at one of the machines. Before I began my search, prickles of anxiety traveled across my upper back, and I turned my head to glance around the room. A handful of people were engrossed in their private tasks. Irrational fears had surfaced about someone maybe watching me. I shook my head. Crazy. These were just leftover feelings from back then. Straightening up in my seat, I scanned the articles from June 1968 and at first found nothing new to me. And I was pleasantly distracted noting the advertisements of the time:

"A-Line floral print summer frocks, $19.99."

"Denim Espadrilles, $6.99."

"Sunbeam Steam Iron, $7.99."

Then, on page 25 of the *Grand Rapids Chronicle* was an article speculating on Sirhan's whereabouts over the years. What jumped out at me was the possibility that he had been seen in northern Michigan in the fall of 1965. That was just 120 miles away from here! Yes! Finally, a reference putting him in Michigan.

Chapter Fifteen

Polka Dots, Polka Dots, Polka Dots

After printing out the new article, I transferred my belongings to a maple table in the corner next to an arched window that looked down on Library Street. Was I hiding? Ridiculous. No one knew this story but me. No one had had this experience but me. It was almost fifty years later. *Get to work!*

In my folder was a copy of the LA Police Department report from June 6, 1968, which is on public record. In the middle of this terse report, I found the following text:

> "PRIOR TO SHOOTING, SUSPECT OBSERVED with a FEMALE CAUC, 23–27, 5'6", WEARING A WHITE VIOLET DRESS, 3/4 INCH SLEEVES, WITH SMALL BLACK POLKA DOTS, DARK SHOES, BUFFAUNT HAIR."

The report had obviously been written by a male. How can a dress be "white violet?" A later article on this report stated that the dress was "white voile," which better described the fabric of the dress. And the word for her hairstyle, *bouffant,* was misspelled.

I became obsessed with finding out all I could about this girl. The best way was through a key witness. After over an hour of reading and looking at pictures, I felt that I knew this important witness. She had been twenty at the time and employed as a keypunch operator. Boy that was certainly a job from the dawn of computer technology! In Pasadena, this key witness had co-chaired the Youth for Kennedy Committee. She and some friends had arrived at the Ambassador Hotel, hopefully to celebrate. While waiting for the final election results, she left the crowded ballroom to escape the heat, and she sat on a fire escape.

This witness said that at eleven thirty, three people tried to get by her on the stairway going up. She moved over for a man whom she would say later was Sirhan Sirhan, a Mexican-American man in a gold sweater, and a pretty girl in a polka-dot dress. About half an hour later, while she was still on the steps, she thought she heard a car backfire. Then the girl in the polka-dot dress and the man in the gold sweater ran out onto the fire escape and past her, almost bumping into her.

"We shot him! We shot him!" the young woman shouted almost triumphantly.

"Who did you shoot?" she asked.

"Senator Kennedy" was the reply.

In a state of shock, she went back inside. A guard in a gray uniform was just inside the door. They were a floor below the hotel's kitchen.

"Is it true they shot him?" she asked.

"Shot who?" asked the guard.

"Senator Kennedy."

The guard thought she was crazy. "I think you've had a little too much to drink, honey."

But this young woman knew what she had heard. She found a public phone booth and called her parents collect, who lived in Ohio. Crying hysterically, she tried to tell her mother what had happened. Just then, a girl she knew came out of the hotel and was outside the phone booth.

"Has Kennedy been shot?" this witness asked her.

"Yes" was the answer.

I felt so sorry for this witness. She had just happened to be cooling off on the exact stairway that Sirhan had taken to commit this murder. And I had just happened to be the one on Lincoln Street whom Sirhan had chosen to stalk. I dug deeper into her saga as a witness.

She found herself in a witness room at one thirty a.m. and suddenly was being interviewed by esteemed NBC television reporter Sander Vanocur. She was visibly upset but seemed clearheaded. Vanocur was gentle and told her to take her time. She told him what had happened and added that she remembered everything the girl had on and that the one young man was Mexican American. She told Vanocur that the girl was Caucasian. She had been wearing a white dress with black polka dots. She was light skinned and had dark hair. She had black shoes on, and she had a funny nose. She claimed it was a "Richard Nixon or ski-jump" nose. Apparently, all her friends said this girl was very observant.

The poor girl was questioned by the LAPD at 2:35 a.m. and later at 4 a.m. The FBI interviewed her the next day, as did the Secret Service. I can imagine how dazed, tired, and overwhelmed she was, yet all accounts had her consistent with remarkable detail. Two days later, she was back at the Ambassador to reenact what had happened for the FBI, police, and Secret Service. The next day, FBI agents interviewed her once more.

The next stop was the police department for her to determine whether Kathy Sue Fulmer, one of a list of women that the FBI would provide, was a possible innocent polka-dot dress girl. Fulmer had informed police that she had been at the hotel wearing an orange polka-dot scarf. Of course, the witness said right away that this was not the woman. On June 10, investigators from the three agencies interviewed her again and filmed her acting out the events she had witnessed.

For some reason, the authorities worked very hard to poke holes in this particular witness's account. From what I've read, the LAPD's task was to break their key witness, and the polka-dot dress woman would be forgotten. One policeman got her, through badgering, to say the word "gunshots" one time instead of "car backfiring." She was grilled about this later. She said she did not mean "gunshots" and didn't even know what a gunshot sounded like. The police knew that gunshots were not heard outside the hotel that night. Boy! This young woman had come forward immediately, didn't vary on any of her details, and was called sincere by a district attorney However, even after other witnesses' testimonies were the same as hers, police notes on June 6 and June 7 stated that her polka-dot story was a phony one.

In 2006, she gave her first interview since the assassination, recounting all that had happened that night. She recalled being treated like a criminal even though she was just telling what she had seen. The LAPD had made her afraid for her safety and told her not to make a spectacle of herself. One sergeant who gave the polygraph test was particularly mean and manipulative, getting her to twist her words and stumble.

In the 1970s, she worked in Latino politics. At every rally, a man stood in the back of the room, staring at her. Finally, at another event, she stared back at him, and he sort of laughed and left. She later found out that the man was the same sergeant who had questioned her and given her the lie detector test. A politician told her that some people felt the man really was maybe FBI or CIA. It took her a very long time to stop worrying about her safety. I could certainly relate to that.

Another campaign worker showed the authorities the polka-dot dress she wore that night, and it was decided that she was probably the one people had seen. However, this dress had large yellow polka dots on orange fabric, where the witnesses all described the dress as small black dots on a white background.

How clear was all this! I felt such sympathy for all that key witness had gone through. I could never figure out why the LAPD was so set against finding the truth. Why did they want to stick to the theory that Sirhan acted alone?

Other sources told of a Jewish couple in their late fifties who approached a police sergeant in a rear parking lot of the hotel, below the stairs where the key witness was sitting. The couple were both talking at the same time and were hysterical. They certainly had not had time to make up their story, as far as I could see. After the officer calmed them down, the woman told him that they had been in the Embassy Room of the hotel and a young, well-dressed couple—the girl had on a polka-dot dress—flew past them very happy, screaming, "We shot him! We shot him!"

The woman asked, "Who?"

The young woman answered, "Kennedy! We shot him! We killed him!"

The officer wrote down the older couple's names, address, and the information and gave the memo to a courier to take it to headquarters. He remembered them as "the Bernsteins."

But no record of his memo was ever found. Really? I wondered what became of them. Had they followed the trial? Had they ever tried to contact the authorities later? Something told me that "Bernstein" was not their last name. I bet it was just a typical Jewish name the officer gave them. And they couldn't still be alive, so I will never know.

A student at Santa Monica Community College was working as a waiter part time at the Ambassador Hotel. His father was a maître d' there and called his son to come to the hotel to see Senator Kennedy. The college student was near the senator as he shook the busboys' hands. The student saw an attractive woman standing next to a young man (later identified as Sirhan). He said they were smiling at each other and whispering. The girl had a good figure and a "pudgy" nose and was wearing a dress with either black or purple polka dots on it. When I examined the trial notes later, it was evident to me that the prosecutors had made sure to trip this young man up during his testimony. So much had happened to him in those minutes in the kitchen, and enough time had elapsed between his accounts to the police and the trial, that I can see how he would appear confused. His eyewitness account was pretty much dismissed during the trial.

I became increasingly fascinated by other witnesses' descriptions of this girl—a part of my thread. A twenty-one-year-old college student was just outside the double doors leading to the hotel pantry when he heard gunshots, and he saw a woman in a black-and-white, polka-dot dress running out. Yes, he heard her say, "We killed him!" as she raced onto a terrace outside. A thirty-three-year-old campaign organizer had been watching Frank Mankiewicz, Kennedy's press secretary, giving an interview at about eleven thirty in the pantry area. He saw a man on the fringe of the crowd whom he would later say was Sirhan. A girl in a white dress with black polka dots and a great figure was standing near him. As I delved deeper into learning all I could about the major witnesses, I couldn't help wondering—although I am no lawyer—how Sirhan's defense team could have let so much of the evidence that Sirhan did not act alone just slip away.

I then pored over the accounts of eight other people who had reported seeing a young woman either with Sirhan, in suspicious circumstances, or running from the hotel. With very few discrepancies, the reports were that this infamous girl in the polka-dot dress was in her early twenties, about five feet seven inches tall, and shapely, with long dark blond or brown hair, brown eyes, and a "pudgy," "funny," or "pug" nose. So, who was she? Could she be the White Rapids College student who had left school to work on RFK's campaign? And, if so, could that thread be looped around me?

So much information swirled around in my head. My eyes were blurry, and I was very hungry. Time to pack up all my stuff. I piled on the heavy clothes to fortify me on my way to the parking lot. The snow and piercing wind had mercifully stopped, and a pale-yellow sun was halfway out from behind a cloud. The air was still frigid, and the inside of my nose crackled, but the walk to the car was a bit easier than the morning trek had been.

Chapter Sixteen

Does the Girl Equal the Girl?

Throughout the week, I couldn't shake the idea of a connection between the girl in the polka-dot dress and the WRC student who had worked on RFK's campaign and me. The idea forming in my mind was that the two young women were one and the same. After all, Sirhan had been in Grand Rapids all those months he stalked me. She had attended college classes in our same town. Could they have possibly ever known each other here? What connection could they have?

Witnesses had spotted the girl in the days before the assassination, during the evening of the killing, and in the pantry, the site of the killing. In the pantry, the witnesses reported her and Sirhan standing on a stack of cafeteria trays, whispering to each other, and helping each other balance. The Mexican-American man who had entered the hotel with them wasn't spotted after that. Where had he disappeared to? Who knows?

I knew the film with all the photographs the young high-school student had taken would have shown exactly where they all were. After Sirhan was convicted, the LAPD destroyed over twenty-eight-hundred photographs along with many pieces of evidence such as ceiling tiles and door jambs with bullet holes in them. What exactly would all that have proved? But alas! Remember? The film was stolen from an agent in a carjacking. I shook my head so many times throughout the research process. What had been going on? How deep did all this go? At the same time, it was becoming clearer to me that a college professor at WRC had been very important to this young college girl. Why else, even after she missed a semester of classes, would she return to see him first after the death of RFK? Sure he taught political science classes, but this man did much more than that at the college. I had been investigating his involvement in something unbelievably sinister, and he had lived a few blocks from me. Did Sirhan know him also?

In 1968 I had noted the college girl's name in the article featuring her in the *Grand Rapids Chronicle.* Placing the newspaper on my lap, I Googled her name, Elaine Peters, and her information, and I now know where she lives today: Michigan City, Indiana. But I was at first more interested in the fact that she had attended high school in Battle Creek. With this information, I was on the phone immediately.

"Good morning, West Battle Creek High School. How may I help you?"

I squared my shoulders, put on an inquiring and guileless voice, and began.

"Good morning. I'm a cousin of one of your graduates, and I'm compiling a surprise photo album for her. I live out of state and can't get my hands on her yearbook. I wonder if you could help me?"

"I can try. What year did she graduate?"

"1966."

"Oh my! No wonder you're having a hard time. That's a while back. I'll see what I can do. It's between classes now, and students are lined up at my counter. I'll try to get back to you today."

"Thank you very much."

I paced around my breakfast room, stopping to gaze at this snow-sculpture garden that was my backyard. I needed to see a picture of this girl. Of course, no photographs existed of her from the time of the 1968 killing, but I surely had enough descriptions from all the witnesses. Hair color was about the only thing on which they disagreed. What color her hair had been in high school didn't concern me; I needed to scrutinize her face.

Refilling my old Tigers mug, I felt too jittery to do much more. But then, who knew when the woman would call back? I went into my office and turned on my prized possession, an exquisite Tiffany lamp. I decided to continue checking out the legitimacy of some of my Internet sources. Two hours later I was ripping up a printed article from an obviously bogus source, and the phone rang. The jitters returned as I slowly stood up and answered. "Hello?"

"Hello. This is Cheryl from West Battle Creek. I was not able to locate the yearbook for you. But perhaps you might be able to find a copy at the Battle Creek Historical Society. Here's their phone number. Give them a call. They should be able to help."

"Thank you so much," I told her.

"No problem. Good luck with your project."

I called the historical society immediately, and a man named George answered. I told him I was looking for a yearbook from West Battle Creek High School, 1966. He replied that it would take him some time to find out but that he would call me back.

My next call was to Seamus, asking him if he had time for a road trip to the Battle Creek Historical Society.

"It is really important because they might have a copy of the yearbook of our White Rapids College student."

"Really, Mom? Of course. Any day next week except Wednesday. Just let me know. This is pretty cool."

"Thanks, Seamus. Love you lots. Bye for now."

Two days later George finally called and said he had located the yearbook I wanted. Breathlessly, I told him we would see him next Tuesday.

"Good. Look forward to meeting you. We open at ten o'clock and close at four o'clock."

Waiting those five days until Tuesday was difficult. I tried to keep busy. One afternoon having coffee at Starbucks with my sisters, Joni and Carol Ann, I mused about how lucky I was to have family around. Everyone in my life from back in the sixties, if they hadn't passed away, still lived in Grand Rapids. Some were still in their original homes, now renovated at least twice. Some had moved a block or two away; some to the other side of town. A phenomenon in Grand Rapids is that the vast majority of those born here do not leave. Our daughter, Anne, was the first in the family to move when her husband, Steve, took a job with McDonald's in the Chicago area. And now my grandson, Tony, and his wife and my first great-grandchild, Natilee, are moving to Denver. Certainly not my preference. But I've been lucky to have my own supportive group of family and friends all these years.

Finally, that Tuesday morning, Seamus and I began our adventure in detective work early and stopped halfway to Battle Creek at a Cracker Barrel. We walked by all those wooden rockers on the porch, and I wondered if anyone ever bought one. At ten thirty we arrived at the museum, a large, modern, gray, L-shaped structure. We searched out George, who was ringing up a purchase. When I introduced myself, he remembered me right away and walked us to the back of the building and up the stairs. The shelves of yearbooks took almost the whole area but were clearly labeled. I told him we would have to make some copies.

"No sweat. Just bring what you need to the desk."

Seamus and I perused the stacks until I cried, "There it is! There it is, but I can't reach it."

Easily retrieving it, Seamus handed me our prize: a maroon yearbook with *West Battle Creek High School Magistro 1966* embossed in gold. I ran my hand over the nubby surface. Biting my lip, I flipped through the glossy pages to find the graduating seniors section. Disappointment greeted me as I saw how tiny these photos were—only about two inches by one and a half inches.

"Look how small these are, Seamus. How will we tell if it's her?"

"We will, Mom. Just keep looking for her."

I found my way down to the *P*s. Down on the middle of the page and to the right, there she was, with her hair back-combed into an exaggerated flip, an OK face, and a wide nose with nostrils more visible than most. Yes. A wide, turned-up nose. This was certainly her. Maybe Sirhan's accomplice. Or was I just hoping? I stared at the photo for several minutes. Then I made five additional selections of girls with similar characteristics. Seamus checked the 1964 and 1965 books for anything interesting and chose three pages with Elaine Peters on them, but in these photos her face was even smaller than the senior shot. I hugged the yearbooks as we went downstairs to make the copies.

Back at home that afternoon, I called the closest Kinko's and asked if they could copy and enlarge yearbook photos for me today and put them all on one page. The clerk replied, "Of course. It would be better if you came in after seven tonight because it won't be busy then, and I'll have more time to spend on your project."

I could hardly wait until evening to head downtown. The same gal who had answered the phone, Lisa, took the photocopies from me and exclaimed, "West Battle Creek High School! My mom graduated from there. What a coincidence!"

"Really?" I said, my chest tightening. "When was that?"

"1966."

Of course. Lisa was only in her twenties. Her mother couldn't possibly have known Elaine Peters. What was the matter with me?

"Could you copy and enlarge the ones I have marked? And I'd like them all on one page. I just want the faces to be clearer. I'm surprising my cousin with old pictures. She'll get a kick out of this."

"OK. I'll try and enlarge it, but not too much or it will be too blurry."

As Lisa pulled the paper with the combined pictures from the copy machine, a coworker glanced at the page and said, "Whatcha got there? Looks like mug shots to me."

My blood turned to ice. A mug shot? Of a criminal? Unsubstantiated rumors had claimed some individuals who had tried to expose the truth about the assassination had ended up dead. What was I doing? Maybe I should forget the whole thing.

I calmed myself down and said, "Yeah, the quality of the picture is pretty bad, but I need it for a surprise."

"Fun," said the coworker and walked to another counter.

Once out of the shop, I scrutinized the photograph. This was unequivocally Elaine Peters. Now that I had identified her, my self-talk needed to be firm. I recommitted myself to the ever-present question of "Why me?" And I knew the answer rested with two people: Elaine Peters and Professor Burgman. There was only one person I knew of who could identify the girl in the polka-dot dress.

The next morning, I attempted to contact this key witness to the mysterious polka-dot dress girl. From my research process, I had found this witness's employment contact information. I called her place of business and left a message. I also personally wrote her a letter explaining that I thought I found the girl in the polka-dot dress and needed to talk to her. Months later she returned my call and initially was very friendly. I began explaining that all I wanted her to do was look at my picture of the mysterious girl. Click. She hung up. My shoulders slumped as my heart sunk. That avenue was closed.

Chapter Seventeen

This Young Man

I had always been terrified by my stalker. Interestingly, the term "stalker" was not even used in the sixties; instead the accepted word was "prowler." Prowler might seem more benign, but it definitely was not. I was horrified that he was the killer of Robert Kennedy. To me and to other Americans, he was a monster, a stealer of our dreams, a lone maniac who had wiped out the life of a man who might have changed history. Many of us believed that.

But who was this young man who had skulked around the streets of Grand Rapids in 1966? I found several sources that had Sirhan at just five two or five three. Janet and I returned to my old house on Lincoln and measured the window. Sure enough, five three put his head in the exact spot where his face was that night in my window. I was sure this was another thread. Chilling.

All accounts of his life agree on his biography. He was a Palestinian Christian, a Jordanian citizen who had lived in Jerusalem during turbulent times. He had experienced constant military fighting and terrorist attacks as the Arab and Israeli sections of Jerusalem battled each other from the time Sirhan was three years old until the family left the country. As a young child, he had witnessed a group of people blown up while they waited for a bus. The most traumatic of all, though, was seeing his older brother run over and crushed to death by a truck that was trying to dodge sniper fire.

When Sirhan was twelve, his father brought his wife and six children to Pasadena, California, through the sponsorship of a minister. They lived with the minister's family for a few months, until the minister found and furnished a home for them. The Sirhan family continued to practice their Christian faith. Sirhan's mother secured a job as a housekeeper for a nursery school, and the children enrolled in the public schools. But Sirhan's father could not adjust to this new culture. He was tense and unsettled and often would beat Sirhan and his siblings. In less than a year, the man abruptly left his family without even telling them and returned to Jordan.

When I was Sirhan's age as a young child, I lived a Norman Rockwell life in Grand Rapids with a loving and supportive father and mother. As Sirhan was physically and emotionally terrorized by political violence, we were in fear of a remote Russia and its leader who would "bury us," but we never lived under constant dread of physical attacks.

At his junior-high school, Sirhan was a serious and quiet young man who endured teasing about his name and ethnicity. Middle Easterners were rare north of Los Angeles at that time. An anecdote had Sirhan going to speak to the principal about his brother being bullied; he had taken the role of the parent. The principal remembers him coming to his office occasionally to chat. I sighed after learning this. Junior high can be difficult for so many kids, not to mention when one is an immigrant *and* a surrogate father at that age.

A few years later, Sirhan's sister contracted leukemia, and he spent months taking care of her. He could not get over the tragedy of her death. His father had deserted him, and now his young sister had left him also. Sirhan had the markings of a lonely soul. He did not date or attend dances in high school. Girls said he was very nice but said they would feel funny dating him.

Almost everyone I had encountered in my young life was just like me and my family, watching black-and-white TV, playing outside until the streetlights came on, going to church, and having daily family dinners with extended family coming over on Sundays after church. I never had to experience being different, an outsider. I had been comfortable with everyone in high school and was even elected homecoming queen.

After graduation from high school, Sirhan attempted college. He wasn't very political, yet he wanted to be a diplomat. He delved into studying languages but was a very poor student and finally flunked out.

At that age, I was falling in love, getting married, and starting our family. Surrounded by my immediate and extended family and so many friends, the word *lonely* never entered my mind.

Pursuing a love for horses, Sirhan worked in a stable, at first for free. In his mind, his slight frame suited him perfectly to become a jockey. After attempting that career, it became apparent that he didn't have the skills necessary, and he eventually became part of a group of horse trainers. One foggy morning, he and three others were racing around the track. The horses couldn't really see, became confused, and crashed into one another. Sirhan sustained a head injury and saw doctors for months, complaining about constant pain, blurry vision, and anxiety. In November 1966, he quit his job and then tried to get it back a month later, to no avail. After that, his official whereabouts become very sketchy until September 1967. But

I know he was in my neighborhood, on my street, and at my home from approximately January to May 1966.

My dreams had been to raise a family and also to contribute to our family's goals. I had the skills to help out on the business end of our shop, and I later became successful in real estate and helping run our sport/entertainment complex. I never felt I was a failure or rudderless.

Sirhan's life circumstances had been so terribly sad and so radically different from my own. But I could not reconcile his background with his violent and unconscionable behavior in June 1968. There had to be more to this young man.

Chapter Eighteen

Theories and a Theory and Me

Anyone can read books, check out the Internet, or read periodicals and discover the same set of theories surrounding the killing of Robert Kennedy. My thread began to encircle one of these theories, not counting our polka-dot dress girl, bringing that thread even closer to me. Curled up in the corner of the couch in the family room, I rechecked my notes and considered all I knew about a possible second gunman. A ballistics expert had stated that the fatal shot to Kennedy was from approximately two inches behind his left ear. Three shots were also fired from close range behind Kennedy. Witnesses had Sirhan in front of the senator. Then maybe Sirhan's bullets were not the ones that actually killed Kennedy?

In the 1970s, the LA Supreme Court had said that there was no evidence to support a second gunman. But as we all know, technology marches on. In 2007, analysis by a forensics expert of a freelance reporter's audio recording of the gunfire that night showed that at least thirteen bullets were fired, and it was known that Sirhan's gun held eight. When I found this out, right away I wondered if the second gunman might not have been the security guard. Could it have been the Mexican-American man who entered the hotel with Sirhan and the girl and then ran out of the hotel with the same girl? A witness testified that he saw a man with a partially concealed pistol in his hand running from the hotel. Could this man and the girl have split up? Since they were never caught, we will never know.

Even though I lived through that fateful day and its aftermath, I did not realize that five other people were shot in the pantry, none resulting in fatal wounds. Ira Goldstein, nineteen, was an intern radio reporter. He shook hands with Senator Kennedy and then was shot in the hip. He felt that he was followed by the Secret Service for several months after the killing. A Mr. Weisel, thirty, worked for ABC News and was shot in the stomach. He continued to work at the White House Bureau but said that people whispered in corners about him taking the second bullet. He eventually left politics to open a bed and breakfast. An activist in the Democratic Party, Elizabeth Evans, forty-three, was grazed by a bullet on the forehead as she bent down to retrieve a shoe. A campaign volunteer, Irwin Stroll, seventeen, was shot in his left leg. His parents watched him on television stumbling out of the kitchen with blood staining his pants. He became a successful interior designer. Paul Schrade, a close friend of Kennedy's, was the director of the United Auto Workers' Union and Kennedy's labor advisor. He was shot in the forehead and miraculously survived. Mr. Schrade successfully campaigned for a school to be built in honor of Senator Kennedy on the site of the Ambassador Hotel. He has also led a decades-long investigation into the second gunman theory and is legally pursuing the case today. But it seems that anyone who remembers that day does not remember that there were other victims. Maybe we were all too much in shock to absorb all that happened.

I dreaded checking out the theories on any CIA operatives' involvement. With JFK and now with RFK, I just did not want to believe in a conspiracy. And selfishly, I feared being personally involved with the CIA. Ever. But I had nowhere to go that day and no excuse to stop working. Eventually and thankfully, I accepted the conclusion among most sources that any evidence trying to connect the CIA, juicy though it sounded, was based on hearsay and fuzzy, inconclusive photographs. There were just too many discrepancies. And let's leave it at that.

Anytime the *Manchurian Candidate* theory popped up in a book, I marked the pages but only skimmed them, or I copied the information from other sources and tossed the copies in a pile on the floor near my desk. During those times, this stuff didn't even warrant a folder. I was vaguely familiar with the old movie of the same name and very skeptical of any kind of far-fetched mind-control idea, and I wanted to keep the lid on that box. But the time had come to open it and adequately explore that theory too.

Video Villa One was the only brick-and-mortar movie rental establishment that I knew was still open. Video Villas Two, Three, and Four had long closed. The day I called the store, the temperature was thirty-eight degrees. There was not a hint of wind, and the sky was a bright, almost Caribbean blue. I checked and found out that the store had a copy of the original *The Manchurian Candidate*, and I decided to walk the mile or so to pick it up. No downhill ski clothes today. Just my white puffy jacket, brown earmuffs and gloves, and comfy UGGs. I spent most of my walk in the street along the curbs because not all the sidewalks were shoveled decently.

Louie, the man who had made a killing as the first guy on the block to sell VCRs and rent movies, still owned and worked the one store he had left. No one really understood how he stayed in business. Just the other snowy Saturday, the Red Box at the Ace Hardware had a long line of customers, to say nothing of Direct TV, Netflix, and the like. Video Villa One was empty of patrons when I entered, and Louie was at the desk, my DVD in hand. I took off my gloves and earmuffs and placed them on the Plexiglas counter.

"I take it that's for me," I said, and smiled at him.

"Yep. Sure is. This is the 1962 original. The Chairman of the Board, Frank Sinatra, is one of the stars. And Angela Lansbury was nominated for an Academy Award. Quite the political thriller."

"So I've heard. I've never seen it. And this is a perfect day for a walk and a movie."

"Well, you know, a new version came out. In 2004, I think. With Denzel and Meryl Streep. You might like that better cuz it was set in the Persian Gulf. Might be more interesting, you know."

"No," I said. "I'm in the mood for an oldie. But thanks anyway."

As I walked home, I reflected on how many business niches folded as times changed. Milkmen became near obsolete as milk and other dairy products became available in supermarkets and corner stores. Small-appliance repair shops closed as our toasters, irons, and radios were made so much cheaper and were easily replaced when they didn't work. And one has to search high and low for a shoe repairman. As a teenager, I remember taking my penny loafers to a crusty old guy in a sweaty sleeveless T-shirt and baggy pants, with a cigar hanging out of his mouth, to have new heels or soles put on—probably at least twice before buying new ones. Anyway, I was happy Louie had still been open for me today.

A few blocks into my walk home, I spotted a policeman through the window at Starbucks. He was seated at a table working on his iPad. Not really planning what to say to him, I walked into the coffee spot. A long line of customers wove through the tables to the counter. The air inside was steamy and smelled like wet wool. I slowly approached the policeman. His sunglasses were pushed back into his wavy salt-and-pepper hair, and he was bent over typing with one finger.

"Excuse me, officer. May I talk to you a minute?"

Startled, he sat up in his chair and blinked at me. "Certainly. What can I do for you? Have a seat." He pushed the opposite chair out with his foot, and I sat down, taking off my gloves and earmuffs and unzipping my jacket.

"Well," I began, "I'm writing a detective-type novel, and I wondered if I could ask you about a particular police procedure."

"Sure. I don't have to be back in the car for about twenty minutes. What's your book about?"

"A young woman who was the victim of a stalker—more like a peeping tom. I'm curious about what police do today when a woman calls about something like that."

He leaned a little closer, and there was sincerity in his intense brown eyes. "We take that very seriously. In fact, I'm part of that very division. A huge percentage of peeping cases end up with a sexual assault. So we stake out the home and a few blocks' radius with unmarked cars or even ride a bicycle by. We stay within the time frame of the incidents because the guy usually has a pattern—like trying to see in a window when the victim is undressing or coming out of the bathroom in a towel. And if there are several incidents, we ask the victim to check to see if anything is missing from her home. At first, most are sure nothing is gone. But often, when they really search, they'll be missing a pair of shoes or a piece of underwear. Unfortunately, we've had some pretty serious cases of sexual assault over the years. But our task force is pretty sophisticated now, and we've arrested a lot of guys before it went beyond peeping. Does any of that help?"

Images from *Law & Order: Special Victims Unit* appeared in my mind. But this wasn't two gorgeous actors in this cop's story. This was cold nonfiction. I became aware of how wide open my eyes were as he added, "Ma'am, did this happen to you?"

"No. Not all of that...just a stalker-type guy looking in my window, banging the doors, watching my house, lurking in the backyard. It all happened over several months, and then it stopped. Plus, we moved. And this was almost fifty years ago. I called the police many times, but they couldn't do anything. There were cigarette butts, footprints, fingerprints—"

"And none of the new technology to help them," he interrupted. "I get it. Luckily, we have tools today. We feel we can protect women and our community much better."

"Thankfully, thankfully. I so appreciate your taking time for me. Have a good day."

"No problem. And I'm glad your experience was minor in the scheme of things."

I grabbed my winter gear but didn't zip up my jacket. I wanted out of there. Outside, the cold air felt good through my blouse and my hair and on the back of my neck. Walking home, I sorted out my thoughts. So, good to know that the police force today was right on about protecting women.

OK. There had been no obvious sexual overtones in Sirhan's behavior. He had that weird blank stare when I first saw him.

At one point, he might have tried to get into our house. And I'm sure I would have known if something had been missing. I had pretty much accepted the idea that I had been chosen simply because it was obvious that I was home alone each night. All the other men on our block worked during the day. And I was by several years the youngest woman there too. But floating around in my consciousness was the idea that Sirhan hadn't been there to just scare me. There had to be more.

Shivering, I realized I had been walking slowly for a while. My pace quickened, and I pulled on my gloves and earmuffs and zipped up.

Back home, mug of coffee in hand, I settled in to watch the DVD. In my family room, the avocado green of yesteryear had been replaced first by the mauves of the eighties and now by neutrals and burgundies. That green rug I had been crocheting when my stalker, Sirhan Sirhan, first appeared in my window had long been given to Goodwill.

The Manchurian Candidate—what a premise! As a prisoner of the Korean War in Communist China, an American soldier is brainwashed to become an assassin and not to remember the details of what happened. Also, two soldiers with him are brainwashed not to remember seeing their fellow prisoner brutally murder two other American captives. The murders take place in front of communist officials who practice their revolutionary brainwashing technique involving hypnotism and drugs. The plot is that the brainwashed American soldier will murder someone when he sees the queen of diamonds playing card. And he has no idea of his capability. One target is the president of the United States. The plan is eventually foiled when the two other soldiers have identical dreams about the murder of the other soldiers, and Army Intelligence becomes involved.

The Manchurian Candidate became more compelling to me as I understood that a huge part of the story was that the subject would not remember who had set him up or why he performed a particular act. But this was just a movie, based on a novel by the same name. I turned off the film and sipped my now-lukewarm coffee, wondering if the truth I was searching for was even stranger than the film.

My glass coffee table was covered with folders and notes and books. I found what I was looking for that perhaps could answer my question. The author of *The Manchurian Candidate* novel, Richard Condon, had interviewed a wide range of experts on mind control in 1959, including a member of a 1953 CIA meeting about mind control. This participant had said that individuals who had come out of North Korea across the Soviet Union to freedom apparently had experienced a blank period of disorientation while passing through a special zone in Manchuria. Fine. Creepy. Frightening. But what about Sirhan? A main part of his defense was that he had been psychologically programmed to kill Kennedy and not to remember the actual shooting or who had programmed him. My initial reaction had been *Really? How convenient*. But I did not know I was headed down a governmental, psychological, conspiratorial path and that the professor in my neighborhood had been connected. He was attached to the thread.

Chapter Nineteen

Mind Control and More

I fell asleep thinking about that movie and woke up doing the same. It was time to examine the pile of papers on the floor next to my desk. It was time to absorb the facts about mind control then and now. It was time to focus on the college professor. The idea of him being involved had been floating at the edge of my thoughts since I read about him back in June 1968. Was this the place where the thread came full circle and could be knotted together?

So much information, conjecture, and mythology swirled around in my brain that I wasn't sure how to tackle this issue. Where should I begin? During my breakfast, I found myself squinting out into the backyard, my hand frozen in air, holding a piece of peanut butter toast. Blinking at the brightness of the snowy blanket outside, I stood up and threw the half-eaten toast into the sink. I retrieved protective pads from the front closet and put them over the dining-room table. On the table, I arranged all the mind-control information from 1952 to the present. I went through it all, highlighting, making notes, outlining, making connections. At one point, I stopped and straightened my shoulders and rolled my head from side to side.

Relaxing a bit, I thought about my fascination with mystery novels: Nancy Drew when I was a little girl, mystery and detective novels by Grisham, Baldacci, Grafton, Larsen, and Dan Brown as an adult. And what about television? *Perry Mason*, *The Rockford Files*, *Law & Order*, *CSI*, and, this season, *Fargo*. All relied on piecing together information and evidence. But that was all fiction. I was working on the truth of my story.

Sanctioned in 1953, a human research project was begun by the US government through a division of the CIA and the army's chemical corps. This project was called MKUltra and sought to control human behavior through mind control. What? Why hadn't I heard of this? I found that in 1975, a congressional committee brought attention to this project. Unfortunately, the then director of the CIA ordered the MKUltra files destroyed. The committee had to rely on sworn testimonies of the participants and on a small number of surviving documents. In 1977, the Freedom of Information Act led to Senate hearings. Today, some information regarding this project is declassified.

So what is known is that many unsuspecting people—prisoners, hospital patients, loners, college students—were used as guinea pigs who did not understand their involvement. Many illegal procedures were used to manipulate the subjects' mental states and change brain functions: hypnosis, the secret administration of drugs such as LSD, sensory deprivation, isolation, abuse. One emphasis was on programming the individuals to commit acts and have no memory afterward of what they had done, who had set them up, or why. A secretary at CIA headquarters was put into a deep trance. One of her coworkers who was deathly afraid of guns was hypnotized.

The coworker was told to try to wake the secretary, and if she didn't wake up to become so angry that she would have to kill her. The coworker picked up a gun left by her boss and "shot" the secretary. After being awakened from her trance, the co-worker remembered nothing about the "shooting." Much has been written about this project, and a documentary has been produced. Everything about this project was horrific and is difficult to read at times. Particularly jarring and now very pertinent to me was the fact that over forty major universities were involved, including one fledgling college, White Rapids College. I knew before I saw his name that the professor involved was the one who had lived around the block from me in 1966, Dr. Leonard Burgman.

I pushed my chair back from the table and deeply inhaled and exhaled several times. Whoa! Whoa! Could this man have sucked Sirhan into the program with the end result being the assassination of Kennedy and Sirhan having no memory of why or who put him up to it? This brought to mind his first interrogation at the LAPD headquarters, when Sirhan asked the officer why he was being arrested. The scenario was too fantastic to believe. Yet, if it was true, Sirhan must have taken the fall for a lot of people. I paced around the house letting this supposition sink in and then ran to my computer. A search showed that the professor was dead. No surprise, since so much time had passed. But Internet articles about White Rapids College, WRC, and the mind-control project included the name of a sitting professor at the university now.

The university website listed names, e-mail addresses, and phone numbers of the faculty members. Great! I might learn something from this man. I called and left a message that I was doing research for a novel and wondered if he could help me.

Within minutes, he returned my call. I told him I was writing a mystery novel set in Grand Rapids, and I was including mind control and the possible involvement of the university. By the sound of his voice, I was pretty sure he was around middle age.

"So, sir, your name pops up on some of these sites."

"That's impossible. I don't know what you're talking about."

"Well, you are a professor there, and—"

He cut me off. "Maybe it's because I'm a well-known speaker in the social sciences. Wait a minute. Are you talking about 1966?"

"Yes."

"Well, White Rapids College didn't even exist then. So you are mistaken."

I paused. "Yes, sir, it did. Not like it is today, certainly. But the beginnings of the campus did exist. There were half a dozen buildings."

"Maybe so. Maybe so. Anyway, I really can't help you. Good luck with your book." *Click.*

I thought the man did protest too much. But I was not going to get any corroboration there.

I thought the whole "Manchurian Candidate" theory, which was decades old, had been debunked. But in the information spread across my dining-room table, I found that the science fiction of that movie is now part of mainstream science. Several experts have testified that it is possible that an individual can be a victim of hypnos-programming and the use of memory techniques, just as portrayed in the movie.

My feelings toward Sirhan Sirhan had moved from very frightened to hatred to sympathy and then to a growing outrage that he had been imprisoned for almost fifty years as the sole killer of Robert Kennedy. I shook my head at these thoughts and read and reread the experts' testimonies from Sirhan's parole hearings every five years. I came to the conclusion that this young man had been a patsy, a diversion. The weight of the knowledge was palpable on my heart. But I had yet to connect the thread to our house on Lincoln Street way back then.

The doorbell rang. It was Anne. She and my granddaughter had recently moved back to Grand Rapids. As a young widow, Anne was now near her immediate family, her close cousins, and old friends. She was ready to begin a new life in familiar surroundings. Fifteen-year-old Paige felt the same and was finally smiling more than she ever had since her dad's death. After our hugs and greetings, Anne headed straight to the kitchen and the coffee pot. With a filled mug in hand, she searched the refrigerator for her favorite hazelnut-flavored International Delight creamer. Leaning against the refrigerator and stirring her coffee, she asked me, "So, what's all over the dining-room table now?"

"Mostly information about all that mind-control stuff. It's really unbelievable. But compelling, too."

"Yeah. That's what you said. But what's this?" She had picked up copies of pages from Sirhan's journals.

"Sirhan's diary. Mostly rantings, gibberish, a lot of 'Kennedy must be killed.' Most of the shrinks said he wrote those things in a hypnotic state. And I keep coming back to the fact that the first date he repeatedly wrote in a notebook was the same date the White River College girl arrived in LA: 'May 18, May 18, May 18'...wow."

"But what could that mean?" Anne asked.

"Was it a coincidence? Or that they were in cahoots? That she was programmed to trigger Sirhan—no insensitive pun intended—to kill Kennedy? I don't know, honey. And there's a lot I won't ever know. But I'm sure they were connected in some way."

"Connected or not, he still did it. Nothing will change that."

"True," I said. "But the more I learn, the more I feel he wasn't solely responsible."

"I know. I know. That's what you keep saying. But after all these years—and if there really is more and more evidence in his favor—why hasn't he been paroled or moved to house arrest or something?"

"Pick up that folder at the edge of the table and look at what I have listed. Wait. Let's get comfy in the family room." Anne sat at the end of the couch, and I sat back a bit in my recliner. The taupe leather was cool at first but warmed as I settled in.

"Anne, how can you be comfortable sitting Indian style like that?"

"Really, Mom, 'Indian style' is not politically correct anymore. Now children say 'crisscross applesauce.'"

"For Pete's sake! What do adults say? Should it be 'Native American style'? Didn't they sit around campfires like that?"

"I don't know, Mom. I just know what's being said now."

"Well, at seventy-four, I'm trying to keep up with so many changes. I'll add that one."

"Good." Anne smiled and said, "OK. Let's see what you have here." She perused the file and began commenting.

"Wow. He's been denied parole thirteen times, always because he didn't show remorse. But it says here that he couldn't do that anyway, since he doesn't remember anything. That's why he requests hypnosis—to try to remember."

"Right," I said. "Now look for the one direct quote I wrote down."

She flipped through the few pages and began to read a statement from an interview with Sirhan in 1993 by author William Klaber.

> I come before the board. I have done well in school, my record is good, but they say I need more psychological tests. Two years later, I have the tests, the tests say I am fine, but then the board wants me to go through the AA program. I haven't had a drink in twenty-six years, but I go through the AA program, and I come back two years later, but now they say they want to see my job offers. Job offers? Just what's supposed to be on my résumé?

She flipped through some more pages and commented on a CNN report.

"So, according to this, psychologists have said he no longer poses a threat to society. And, whoa, one of the men shot by a stray bullet back then told CNN that after reviewing the psychological information, he would not oppose Sirhan's release." Anne closed the folder on her lap.

"OK, Mom. This is sad and crazy and probably unfair. But Sirhan Sirhan did shoot Robert Kennedy. There's no getting around that."

"I know. I know. I'm as surprised as you are that my feelings have changed toward him as I try to figure out how I fit into this whole deal. Nothing about the assassination is what it seemed to all of us in 1968. And I know that no matter how much new evidence is available showing that he was a pawn, Sirhan will never be paroled. I think that too much egg would be on so many influential faces after so many years."

Anne bit the left side of her lower lip and then said, "I can't imagine how many times powerful people on so many levels have screwed up cases for all kinds of cover-up reasons. It's too much to get my head around."

"I agree. It's scary. But at this point, I can't let all that distract me from finding out all I can to explain what happened to me."

"Do you think that's possible? Finding out your part, I mean?"

"Yes, I do. Because I know what happened to me. And I now know enough about Sirhan in the years before the as-sassination to be pretty sure he wasn't just a typical stalker. Also, there's a strong connection here because an LAPD of-ficer commented on Sirhan's blank stare at the time of the first interrogation. And that stare still haunts me."

"OK, Mom." Anne sighed. "I'll be happy for you when you can come to some sort of resolution for yourself...whatever that will be."

"Thanks, honey. I think I'm closing in on just that."

Smiling, she gave me a huge hug. On her way through the dining room, Anne picked up *The Manchurian Candidate* DVD. "Where did you get this from?"

"Video Villa One."

"I can't believe that place is still open. Mom, you could have downloaded this to your iPad or computer. You should have Netflix too. All much easier."

"Yeah. I should do a lot of things. But I'm perfectly hap-py seeing Louie and really, I enjoyed the walk. Not ready to change that yet!"

"I'm just sayin'. Anyway, I can return this on my way home, if you'd like."

"Sure, Anne. That would be great."

Arm in arm, we walked to the door.

Chapter Twenty

The Professor's Wife

Sunday at Mass, I spotted Marcia Vandermeer, my old neighbor from Lincoln Street. I hadn't seen her in a few years, and she was now in her eighties. Marcia was perched at the end of the first pew with a walker at her side. On my way up to Communion, I patted her shoulder. She looked up at me, her eyes and smile bright with recognition. At the end of Mass, I waited in the vestibule for her. Instead of any final prayers, my mind had jumped at an idea.

Marcia wasn't really using her walker but was just carrying it. Smaller than I remembered, she was smartly dressed in a deep-brown corduroy coat with tan fur collar and cuffs.

"Margo Huver!" she exclaimed. "My goodness. I haven't seen you in so long. Do you always come to this mass?"

"Yes. It's almost always nine thirty for me, but I've never seen you here."

"Oh. I always come to the seven thirty mass. Last night was a birthday party for my daughter-in-law, and I was up pretty late. The woman's sixty. Ya'd think she'd stop throwing parties for herself."

"Well, how are you?" I asked. "Aren't you supposed to be using that walker?"

"My family seems to think I need it, so they bought me one. Ridiculous. I bring it in case I run into any of them. I'm fine. Still in my old house, you know."

"Good for you, Marcia. Are you busy now? Want to get some breakfast?"

"I would love that. My bridge group doesn't start until two. Let's meet at IHOP. I'll bring my walker. Sometimes that gets me to the front of the line."

Soon we were seated comfortably in a booth, sipping coffee and orange juice. Marcia had folded her walker and placed it next to her. We caught up on our families and the fact that so many of our neighbors were dead—some too young, especially Chris, and even her oldest daughter. Marcia's Marv had died about ten years before Butch. We lamented the challenges of widowhood. Then I steered the conversation to back in the day.

"Marcia, remember those months when I was stalked?"

"How could I forget? You poor thing. You were so scared. And nobody ever caught him. Say, I remember hearing that you thought it was the guy who killed Bobby Kennedy. I figured that wasn't true."

"It was true. It is true. And I am now trying to figure out why."

"But that was so long ago. How can you learn anything now?"

"You'd be surprised how much information is available about the whole assassination....Way too much to go into."

The waitress brought us our breakfast and refilled our coffee cups. I continued.

"When I saw you in church, I remembered that you had a cousin who lived next to that college professor around the corner from us."

"Right. A Professor Burgman. He's dead, you know. My cousin moved. Married a ne'er-do-well and moved to the UP. She—"

I interrupted her because I knew how long winded she could be when dishing about someone. Personalities really don't change.

"Marcia. What do you remember about the guy? Married? Children?"

"I don't know much, but Flo in my bridge group, her husband is in the nursing home just west of Wyoming. She said she sees Mrs. Burgman, another resident, now and then. Says the woman is pretty looney. What does she have to do with anything?"

"Well, I have a theory that her husband was connected to Sirhan."

"Theory? What theory? Tell me all about it."

"I don't have any real proof yet, and I thought if I could maybe talk to his wife—"

"I told you. She's looney. You'll get nothing from her."

"Marcia, I plan to try. What's the name of the place?"

"Glade Haven. How's that for a name? Just like the rest of them around here—Golden Living Community, Whispering Pines, Good Samaritan Village. Who do they think they're kidding? I prefer the old 'God's Waiting Room.' Not for me. I plan to croak right on Lincoln Street."

I smiled. "I hope that works out for you."

As we finished our breakfast, I couldn't concentrate on Marcia's chatting. I needed to work on connecting my thread.

A billboard picturing a well-tanned, attractive, silver-haired couple being served dinner in a lovely dining room advertised the Glade Haven Homes along the freeway. I had driven by it many times, but now I paid attention to the freeway exit number on the sign. As I drove, I pictured episodes from *Columbo* or *Mannix* or *Cannon* or any other detective show from the seventies. The protagonist would be walking on a lush lawn with an officious nursing-home employee, speaking about the resident they were about to meet. The elderly person would be sitting in a wheelchair with an attendant, male or female, who was dressed in white. The resident, with an afghan on his or her lap, would be gazing blankly into the distance. And here I was embarking on the same mission as those detectives. But again, this was no television drama.

Glade Haven Homes, founded 1941 was engraved on a large granite marker at the entrance to the establishment. This looked too much like a gravestone for me. It probably wouldn't have years ago, but now that I was in my seventies, things had a different tint. After checking online, I knew that the first building was for independent living. This one-story deep-red brick structure looked like so many motels years ago on two-lane highways that boasted "Air Conditioned" and "Color TV" in neon pink. Each white door had a white, plastic molded chair in front on a tiny patch of lawn. That material can exist through any season. These chairs had an extra layer of white right now—snow.

The road curved toward the right, to the assisted-living area. The two-story, light-red brick building was attractive, with peaked roofs over every other unit. Balconies bordered with white-spindled railings jutted out along the second floor. The units without balconies had tall blue spruce trees near the sidewalk.

I slowly drove around the arced road past a small area with park benches and a dormant fountain ringed in that slate-gray granite. At the end of the cul-de-sac, set back thirty yards or

so, stood the nursing-home facility. The long three-story building was white brick with black shutters and a hunter-green
door. Interesting to me was that the worse one's health became, the more attractive was the exterior of one's building.

I parked in the lot at the far right and followed two workers, whose maroon scrubs showed beneath their coats, into
the building. I would later learn that the color of the scrubs
indicated the occupation of the employees. Maroon was for
the orderlies who changed the linens, dressed the residents,
and helped them in and out of bed and into wheelchairs—in
other words, they did the heavy lifting. Powder blue was for
the nurses, pink for the clerical workers, and white lab coats
over street clothes denoted the doctors.

The lobby area was soft and soothing, the only light from
lamps on the mahogany tables and a skylight. Floral print fab-
rics of rose and seafoam green covered the furniture. Opposite
the front doors was a semicircular cherry wood counter. As I
approached it, the receptionist removed her turquoise reading
glasses and smiled up at me.

"Good morning. How may I help you?"

"I'm here to visit Mrs. Burgman."

"Ah yes, Grace. She's been here so long that I don't have to
look up her room number. That's room 324. Take the elevators
to your left. Feel free to help yourself to coffee and cookies."

"Thank you very much."

Next to the reception desk was a cart holding a tall copper
coffee urn, the ubiquitous Styrofoam cups, powdered cream
containers, and sweetener packets of various colors. A glass
pedestal plate of homemade oatmeal raisin cookies under a
plastic dome stood next to the urn. I planned to stop here on
my way out. As I stepped onto the elevator, I noted no cloying

floral or nursing-home disinfectant odors. Entering the long elevator from the opposite door were two male orderlies pushing a gurney holding a very elderly gentleman who was sound asleep. The orderlies and I nodded at one another. Silently, they got off on the second floor.

As I stepped off on the third floor, there was the scent of disinfectant. Beneath it was a fairly masked odor of urine. Wheelchairs lined the wall opposite the stainless-steel sterile nurses' station. No one behind the desk even looked in my direction. The wheelchairs' inhabitants were in various postures. Two were bent over with their heads almost on their laps; some bodies were hanging off the sides of the chairs, and others had their heads thrown back, with mouths open. *Dear Lord! Help these people. Help their families. Help the people looking at them all day. And help me never to have to be here.*

One of the two who were upright looked alert. I gazed directly into her eyes and said, "Good morning."

"Humph," she replied.

I answered with a look that said, "I get it," and followed the signs to room 324.

The nameplates to the right of the door read Harriet Lumpkin and Grace Burgman. I assumed that Harriet would be in the first bed and Grace the second, but I wasn't sure. An orange coverlet embroidered with a large script *L* lay smoothly over the first bed. So I was correct. Harriet's covers lay under her chin, and she was so thin that it looked as if just a head was sleeping there. I quickly stepped around her bed, past the butterfly-print dividing curtain, and into Grace's section of the room.

Instead of the traditional institutional bed frames, here there were curved mahogany ones. Each side of the room had a built-in mahogany chest of drawers with a mirror above it. The closets and bedside tables were of the same rich wood. What belied the appearance of a normal bedroom were the call button and the hospital-style apparatus for raising and lowering the beds. The window near Grace's bed was even covered with a valance of the butterfly print. But under the window stood the ever-present wheelchair.

Some of the residents might have walked in here, but very shortly thereafter, they got deposited in wheelchairs. Did they need them, or was it the workers who needed them to make care easier?

The Price is Right blared from the small flat screen on the wall near the end of Grace's bed, though she was gazing out the window. The woman in the bed was sitting upright and had thin squared shoulders on a medium frame. Her neck was long and slender, and her angled head showed a firm-skinned older face with long crow's feet at her eyes and deep lines on both sides of her mouth, which reminded me of a puppet's. Her hair was a high puffball of white cotton candy, and it was sure to be flat and messy in the back. I reached for the remote on her nightstand and slowly lowered the TV's volume until she looked at me. I hit the off button.

Not startled, she gazed up at me, revealing violet Liz Taylor eyes.

Shyly, she said, "Hello. Am I supposed to know you?"

"No. We've never met. My name is Margo, and I came to visit you."

"Well, that's nice. You're not my sister, are you?"

"No. I'm just a friend."

On the other side of the curtain, Harriet stirred and moaned and then weakly said, "Help me."

I walked over to her and pressed the call button.

"Thank you very much. You must be an angel," Harriet said, and then she resumed moaning.

After a moment, I excused myself politely and stepped into the hall, seeking someone to help her. No one was in sight, even though the red call light was blinking. I walked the thirty yards to the nurse's station and again was not acknowledged. The two nurses didn't look up from their incessant tapping on their keyboards.

"Excuse me? Harriet in 324 needs help. She seems to be in pain."

A bored face on a woman dressed in powder blue glanced up at me and asked, "Are you her family?"

"No. I'm visiting Grace. I'm just trying to help Harriet."

"Well, her caregiver is in another room and will get to her eventually. She probably needs to be turned over."

"Why? Does she have bedsores? Don't you answer the call light?"

Bored Face peered at me. "You're not family, so I'm not at liberty to discuss Mrs. Lumpkin. Don't worry. Someone will get to her."

Frowning and disgusted, I realized that I was pretty powerless and returned to the room. Thankfully, Harriet had fallen back to sleep.

A huge and handsome black man in maroon scrubs came into the room and smiled at me. His name tag read "Jamie."

I asked him,

"Sir, since Harriet's asleep now, could you please get Grace into her wheelchair? I would like to take her down to that sitting room I passed."

"Sure thing." He knelt down and put his face in front of Grace's. "Dear, would you like to get in your chair and go for a ride?" She smiled and nodded. He gently lifted her as if she were a child, settled her into the wheelchair, and slipped fluffy red slippers onto her feet. "This will be nice for Grace. She doesn't usually get visitors."

I shook his hand. "Thank you for your help and for being so sweet with Grace." I was beginning to be protective of her.

"Will you be able to help Harriet now, I hope?"

"Sure. These two ladies are a couple of my charges. There just isn't enough of me to go around—as hard as that might be to believe." He grinned.

His smile was infectious, and I was sure he was wonderful at his job. I returned a smile and wheeled Grace out of her room. I wondered when she had last been out of it, let alone out of this whole place. Luckily, no one was in the sitting room, which was decorated similarly to the lobby. A half-completed jigsaw puzzle covered a card table, and a huge bay window offered a view of the tops of pine trees and a neighborhood of modest Cape Cod–style homes beyond.

I wheeled Grace over to the window and sat next to her, holding her thin, veined hand in mine.

"Grace," I began, "I would love to talk with you about your life. About your husband, Leonard."

"Leo," she said, sitting up straight and looking at me. "Everyone calls him Leo. Just last month, we were on our honeymoon on Mackinac Island. Stayed at the Grand Hotel. Had our breakfasts and dinners on the grand porch overlooking the straits. Walked around the island during the day. No cars there, you know. Ate fudge. Took horse and buggy rides too." She slumped down and looked out the window. "My Leo died.

So sad. I really miss him. He was handsome and so smart. Really smart."

She had just jumped several decades. I had to get her to talk about his college years, though I realized that she might not know anything about his mind-control experiments or anything else that had gone on then.

"Grace, did you enjoy being a professor's wife at Grand River? Were any of your friends the wives of other professors?"

"Friends? Friends? Oh yes. We played jump rope and jacks and pickup sticks on the back porch. My father hung a hammock from the oak trees in the yard..." And then her head dropped again, and she was asleep. I guess I had known this would be a long shot, but I was still disappointed. Sighing, I stood up to wheel Grace back to her room.

Suddenly, another wheelchair came flying into the sitting room. The chair dwarfed the man inside it. His red plaid flannel shirt was tucked into black sweat pants, and he wore bright-red Nikes. His silver hair was reminiscent of Christopher Lloyd's character, Doc Brown, in *Back to the Future.* But his deep-brown eyes behind wire-rimmed glasses were clear and inquisitive.

"Ya talking to Gracie, here? Good luck. I just let her yap and yap. She doesn't make much sense. But she seems a little happier when I visit her. I think she was a looker once. But then so was I. A dapper Jewish dentist, that was me. Yessiree."

"And your name is..."

"Roland. Roland Herbertson."

"A pleasure to meet you, Dr. Herbertson. I'm Margo."

"Please, it's just Roland. You her friend?"

"Well, we just met." I smoothed Grace's hair.

Roland wheeled closer to me and whispered, "Whatever you do, do not mention her basement. She starts talking

crazier than ever and gets all worked up. I'm just tellin' ya."
He checked his watch, which hung loosely on his bony wrist.
"Hey, it's almost time for lunch, and if I'm not in my room,
the maroonies—that's what I call them—will be after me. See
ya." He spun his chair around and, pushing those wheels with
amazing strength, was gone.

I sat back down and turned Grace to face me. She was like
a droopy jack-in-the-box. I gently stroked her face. She raised
her head, opened her eyes, and seemed to recognize me. I
took both her hands in mine and smiled, not knowing how to
broach the subject of the basement. I asked her to describe
her home in Grand Rapids.

She perked up and talked about each room in detail. By the
time she reached the attic, I was impatient.

"Did your house have a basement?"

She stiffened and pursed her lips. She then closed her eyes
but didn't seem asleep. I didn't want to upset her, but I needed
what she might know.

"Grace. It's OK to tell me about your basement. I'm your
friend."

"Too scared. Too scared."

"Why?"

"Don't know. Don't know. Didn't understand. Why couldn't
I look in that file cabinet down there? Why was the closet
locked that was next to the furnace? Don't know. Don't know.
Can't help it."

She was wringing her hands, which were half covered with
her lacy sleeves. I thought she might cry. I wondered what to
ask her next. Keeping her in that timeframe was important.

"You know what, Grace?" I said. "I heard your Leo was a
wonderful teacher. Did you ever meet his students?"

"Oh yes." She perked up. "We would have a tea for them at the beginning of each semester." A litany of what was served followed.

I interrupted with the next question. "Did any students come to your house to visit?"

"Yes. Each term, a few really adored him. They would come over at any excuse.

They were charming, would serve Coke and Tab and lemonade. And pretzel sticks."

I held her eyes with my own, hesitated, and then asked, "Were there any people who came over the most? And did you like them?"

Her features hardened, and she turned toward the window. I wasn't sure if I should continue pushing, but I had come this far. I turned her chair so that she faced me directly.

"Don't worry. This was a long time ago, and nothing can hurt you. I'm just your friend asking you some questions. Who came over the most, Grace? What were they like?"

She slowly looked up at me, with her lips quivering. I tried to remain nonchalant.

"I don't know why I'm afraid. Maybe those two men in the dark suits. Why wear sunglasses in the winter? Sunglasses, both the same, and too dark. Never got their names. And the boy. The small boy. So lonely. But so disturbed all the time. Once, I gave him a warmer jacket. Did he call him Sam? Sometimes he came over at night. I stayed upstairs. Just knew I should."

I couldn't believe what I was hearing and tried not let her see my quickened breath. She had paused and was starting to fade away.

"Grace! Grace! Who else came over a lot? Anyone else?"

"Yes. Later. For some months...a girl. Coeds, we called them." She was back with me, and I asked her to tell me more about the girl.

"She was serious and intense, not a smiler. I guess I might have been a little jealous because she was a looker. Not real pretty, but a curvy figure. And Leo said she was very smart. I always wished I was smart like that. My brothers went to college, but I wasn't even given a chance. Did I tell you how I always played school when I was little? Set up my dolls in folding chairs. My father bought me a blackboard and chalk. My pupils always paid attention." And she was asleep. Just like that.

Oh my God! I plopped down on a nearby love seat and wrote down everything she had just said. Not that I would forget; I just needed to get it down to make sure of everything I had just heard. I underlined key information. Men in dark suits—FBI? The small boy—she gave him a warm coat. Sirhan had worn a lightweight jacket that winter night he'd first looked in my window. The name "Sam"—Sirhan? The shapely coed— the girl in the polka-dot dress, Elaine Peters? This thread was weaving and weaving.

Grace was waking up. "Ain't too proud to beg, sweet darlin,'" she sang. "Stop in the name of love." Motown had invaded her thoughts, and I could not get her back.

As I wheeled her back to her room, she mimicked the others lined up against the wall, falling asleep again and hanging off to the side. I straightened her up and deposited her near the window by her bed.

Harriet was peacefully asleep as I left the room. A pretty doctor in black pointy-toed spike heels was in the hall, leaning against a computer stand and keying in information. I asked her to look in on Grace and Harriet. She assured me that she would. But would she?

On my way through the lobby, I grabbed two cookies and walked to the door. Once inside my car, I digested all that I had discovered today, along with the cookies.

Chapter Twenty-One

Doubts and a Dinner

The next morning as soon as I opened my eyes, a black cloud of dread descended on me. I sat up and shook my head and arms, trying to dissipate it. Didn't happen. I sank back onto my pillow, attempting to put a finger on my feelings. Grace had talked about men in dark glasses, a basement, a file cabinet, a closet, a coed, and a lonely young man. Adding all this to what I already knew about all the cover-ups, bogus carjacking, LA police involvement, MKUltra, the polka-dot-dress girl, and on and on resulted in the proverbial elephant sitting on my chest. If an ordinary woman like me could put these pieces together, surely some authority could do the same? But would any have even checked the *Grand Rapids Chronicle* from back then and seen the two articles about the two young women? Probably not. But they certainly could do it today. And what if they did? Would they want the truth to come out? Most likely not. Someone had too much culpability for deliberately making sure that only Sirhan had been held responsible for the assassination.

These events had been almost fifty years ago, and many of the people involved were not even alive. But suddenly, I was back to my twenty-seven-year-old vulnerable and paranoid self. What about Elaine Peters, the polka-dot girl from

1968, about sixty-eight now, living in Michigan City? Was she guilty? Or had she also been psycho-programmed? Could anything happen to her as a result of my story? Or should it? Many more suppositions and scenarios plagued me as I stayed in my bed.

I found myself gulping for air. For the second time, I sat up. What was that anti-stress technique? *Breathe in to the count of seven; hold my breath to the count of seven; breathe out to the count of seven; repeat seven times.* I did this twice, and I was finally breathing normally. But the elephant was still sitting on my chest. I felt so alone in all this.

I reached for my cell phone and texted my kids. *How about coming for dinner tonight...just you guys...no children or grandkids...at six thirty?* I knew they were all in town and would appreciate the invitation. All the years I was working, I'd been thrilled when my mother invited us for dinner—no planning, no cooking for me. Wonderful.

Within an hour, all had responded with a yes, some of them followed by exclamation points. Anne said she would bring a tossed salad. Great!

Now I needed to figure out what to make. I reached for my Mishy Cookbook. A smile came over my face as I read, *Mishy is a warm feeling among family and friends.* This made me think about all of my family and friends who were so instrumental in helping me through the stalking. The book opened to the page with the picture of Ma and her sisters. The caption below read. *"Life is precious and short and sometimes very tough. Don't sweat the small stuff. Pick your battles. Trust your instincts."* It sure is, I thought. I flipped through the book and found Joni's recipe for lasagna. That sounded good and I was pretty sure I had all the ingredients. With Anne's salad and some warm bread, this will be perfect. Soon the house was filled with the delicious aroma of garlic and seasoning. I pulled out the dishes and began to set the table.I set out the wine glasses and a rich bottle of red. I knew I had some white already chilling in the fridge.

Anne arrived first. I was still not used to seeing her without Steve. Such a bright, beautiful young woman should not be alone. My heart ached for her. A friend had once repeated a statement she'd heard and I agreed with: You are only as happy as your unhappiest kid. This sounded like a life sentence to me then and was certainly not on my radar when Butch and I were having babies. I blocked out these "glass-half-empty" thoughts and hugged my daughter. I took the salad from her, and she followed me into the kitchen, hanging her red swing coat on the back of a chair. After sliding the salad into the back of the fridge, I asked, "How's Paige? What is she doing tonight? What about her dinner?"

"Right now, she's good. She is at long dance practice, and then a bunch of the girls are going to Chili's after. She should get home right about when I do. Since Steve died, Paige isn't that thrilled about being alone in the house." She sighed. "Don't know when we'll truly be back to normal. You did OK after Dad died, right? I know it seems like that to all of us, at least."

"Oh, Anne. I don't know what 'normal' is, really. All I know is that life can be meaningful and enjoyable even after a tragedy. I didn't believe that at first. But now I know it's true. You'll see." We hugged again, tighter this time. I leaned on the breakfast bar.

"Seamus texted that he'd be a little late. He had to clean up something at work. He works so many hours at the shop and has been alone for so many years since his divorce. I worry."

"Maahmm," Anne started. I knew when the word "Mom" got exaggerated that either I had overstepped or she didn't want to talk about the subject.

"It's just that I just can't help worrying about you kids. Even if there is nothing to worry about."

"Don't you know that worrying, especially about things you can't control, can take years off your life?" She smiled at me.

Dan and his wife, Mary, knocked on the door and stepped into the front hall. Dan was now the owner of our shop. He upgraded all the equipment, and was often called to check new equipment installations, and trained people all over the world. Mary was a 3-D CAT Scan expert at the hospital and worked two twelve-hour shifts each week. Luckily, this wasn't one of those days.

"I can't believe I'm not traveling and get to be with everyone for dinner," Dan said as he hung their coats in the front hall closet.

"Amen," Mary added. "This is such a treat, Mom. I looked forward to it all day. We've both been wondering—is this a special dinner or something?"

"Yeah, Mom, you got a boyfriend stashed somewhere to meet us?" Dan, the joker.

"Real funny, Danny. Uncork the wine, please—the red and the white—and pour us a glass while we wait for the others. Hey, Dan, are you making Seamus work too hard?"

"No. I guess we both just have a little of Dad in us...we don't leave until the whole job is done. Seamus volunteered to stay later tonight."

They moved into the family room while I checked the lasagna. Then I brought a pitcher of chilled water into the dining room to pour over ice in the sparkling, cut-crystal goblets that had been a twenty-fifth anniversary gift from our children. I cherished the glasses more than I did our now-antique wedding presents.

Soon, Todd and his wife, Amanda, arrived. They took off their coats and helped themselves to wine, as they joined us.

"Ooh...so great to be here." Amanda said as she plopped into the recliner. "Wonderful to get off my feet." She was a specialist in Internal Medicine in her own private practice who I also thought worked too hard.

"Seamus just texted, he's fifteen minutes away," Todd said. "Mmm. I smell Italian." Todd, an industrial engineer who did contract work for major corporations which needed specific grinding equipment, also traveled internationally and would leave soon for two weeks in China. He stepped behind Anne's chair and rubbed her shoulders.

She closed her eyes, sighed, and smiled.

"So nice. One thing I'm so happy about is being back in Grand Rapids with all you guys. Mary, thanks for suggesting the townhome complex and the perfect subdivision for us. Paige and I love our new home. Now I should learn to play golf."

Seamus tromped into the house and boomed, "Sorry I'm late! I hustled as much as I could."

I ushered everyone into the dining room to pass the salad and garlic bread. I deposited the steaming lasagna into the center of the table and slid a square onto each plate. We prayed the blessing together. Not all there were churchgoers, but this tradition played out at every family meal, no matter where we were.

"A toast to Mom," Seamus said, and we all clinked our glasses. All was quiet for a few moments as we took our first bites.

"Delicious."

"Just the right amount of spiciness."

"Mmmmm."

"This is a different recipe. So good."

"Whose recipe?"

"Love coming here to dinner."

These were all gratifying comments for me. Family and food together—what more could a mother want on this winter evening? Actually, this particular evening, I needed more.

"So..." I began. Six sets of eyes were on me, and forks stopped where they were. I continued. "No, nothing is seriously wrong." There was a symphony of sighs, and the forks were moving again. "As you know, I've been forging full steam ahead with my research, getting down anything I can to make sense of Sirhan stalking me. But the closer I get to piecing all this together, the more freaked out I get—almost like I was all those years ago. Even thinking back to me measuring the window in our old house to make sure that Sirhan's short stature equaled that grease mark on my window—a perfect match—gives me chills."

"What exactly are you afraid of?"

"That was almost fifty years ago."

"Aren't most of those people dead?"

"Is anyone really going to care what one woman in Middle America thinks?"

"It's not like you to not see something through."

"You won't be happy until you come to terms with this whole experience."

"Just take your time."

"Keep using us as sounding boards. So far, nothing has seemed even remotely dangerous to us."

And so on, and so on. Not a negative comment in the bunch. If this had been a scene in a movie, "The Wind Beneath My Wings," Butch's favorite song about me, would be playing.

I gazed around at my children.

"I know all this intellectually. It's just that now and then, I project into the future, or I wonder if any of these people I'm contacting—the professor at White River, for instance—will report what I'm doing to some authority. And when I see how those in charge behaved in the fifties, sixties, seventies, and beyond, I can't help not wanting to become vulnerable to powerful people. Maybe I've watched too much of *The Blacklist* or *House of Cards*."

"Hey, at least it's not *Breaking Bad*!" Dan said.

"Mom, don't you think if any one of us thought this was dangerous, we would ask you to stop and leave well enough alone? Anytime we talk about you and your project, we're interested and excited and in your corner," Amanda said.

"That's true," added Anne. "Everyone we know is fascinated and wants to know more about it and what it all has to do with you and Grand Rapids."

"Well, I want you all to know that if I disappear or am found dead, it will be because of all this," I said.

"Really, Mom?" Anne's eyebrows were raised as high as possible.

"Really. Just a minute. Let me get some notes." I went to my computer and looked through the files that were stacked on the chair. I assumed that those in the dining room were rolling their eyes or frowning or wearing worried expressions. I also grabbed my glasses and then returned to the dinner table.

"Just you guys listen to this, and follow the sequence of events. In 1977, a columnist named Allard Lowenstein wrote an article for the *Saturday Review* about some possible motives for the suppression of evidence about Bobby's assassination."

"What's the *Saturday Review*?" Todd asked.

"I checked it out. The magazine started in the 1920s and critiqued all aspects of American culture. Three years after his article, Lowenstein was shot and killed in his office by a former colleague. This former colleague was called deranged in the press. People who knew the shooter said he was a nut. Maybe he was...handled?"

"More conspiracy stuff, Mom?" Todd said.

"Just wait. Let's see...in 1983, Gregory Stone an investigative reporter, Lowenstein's colleague, wrote a book called *Lowenstein: Courage and Beliefs.* A few years later, he got a committee together to examine the handling of the RFK assassination case, which meant going over thousands of pages of testimony. This committee found numerous items that were wrong and should be tried in court. Before the new trial, Gregory Stone drove to a local park in Washington DC, sat under a tree, and shot himself. Was it really suicide? Why would he do that? This political researcher was so close to wrapping up his findings. Did he find some new damning evidence against someone powerful?" I flipped through some more notes.

The committee decided to keep going with Mr. Stone's quest, and in April 1992, they filed a petition to the Los Angeles County Grand Jury by Paul Schrade, who had been shot and wounded in the kitchen of the Ambassador Hotel where Bobby was murdered. The long document included over eight hundred pages of exhibits that needed investigating by the grand jury. Listen to my list of the concerns of Paul Schrade and the committee that I think is glaring.

"Police records had several statements that more than one gun was fired while Sirhan was shooting.

"Door jambs and ceiling tiles that had showed bullet holes were destroyed.

"More than twenty-four hundred photos were destroyed.

"Bullet casings were substituted.

"And, of course, there was the discounting of many valid witnesses. And you know what? The case was closed with no investigation."

"Man," Mary said. "All of that is incredible."

"Also, as far as Sirhan is concerned, I have found some Los Angeles Police Department connections that I can't help thinking about. An LA detective was said to be with Sirhan at a gun shop buying bullets and again with him at a shooting range the day before the assassination. No more information or follow-up there. A few years previous, Sirhan had been arrested for a petty crime and then released with no explanation. This young man was a loner who as a child witnessed firsthand the atrocities of war and suffered under the hands of an abusive father. He was unsuccessful with women, in college, and in establishing any kind of career. A perfect person to be preyed upon, Sirhan could easily have been recruited for the then-illegal mind-control program. It could be that he was selected for this program at the time he was arrested by the police, and the charges were mysteriously dropped. And maybe then he was sent to Michigan to be part of this sinister program. And I'm telling you guys I am really beginning to feel sorry for him."

"Gosh, Mom, this is really how you feel?" Anne asked, and the others did the same with their eyes.

"Yes. Yes, I do." You want more? I said. "A lawyer on his way to present information on the case to the grand jury was killed in a car accident. Great timing, wasn't it? So that's why I'm still afraid. But I need to get this story out before I die. And, like I said, if it happens in a suspicious manner, I told ya so!"

"Mom, Mom, Mom. None of that is less than twenty years ago. You aren't really bringing out anything that is not really out there," Anne said.

"Not yet," I said.

"But this could all be circumstantial."

"I know, Anne, but it also could be *not* just circumstantial."

"Mom, we all feel you are truly very safe."

The rest nodded or voiced their agreement. I looked at each one. "Thanks." I rested my chin on my folded hands. "I guess now I'm only a little scared. I know I can't quit. I just needed to hear your encouragement again. Yay for you guys. One more toast."

Another clinking of glasses, and we were on to catching up with the grandkids and everyone's job, plus plans for a camping reunion this summer. We eventually took our coffee and cheesecake into the family room. Once we were settled, Dan asked, "So Mom, what's your next step?"

"Well, this could be huge or disappointing." I paused. "Or have consequences."

A chorus of "What?" followed.

"I'm thinking of visiting Elaine Peters, the polka-dot dress girl—I mean woman. Seamus dug around and found out she lives in Michigan City."

"How did you find her, Seamus?" Mary asked.

"The old Google. Evidently she didn't get married, or she kept her maiden name. Lucky for mom."

"Wow, just an hour and a half away from us in Indiana. Exciting!" Mary said. "So, what's your plan?"

"Well, first of all, Anne, will you come with me? There's no way I'm going alone, and you haven't settled on a new job yet."

"Of course. Oooh, Mom, an adventure! How should we go about it? Call first? Knock on her door? Or set up a meeting?"

"I'm not sure. Let me think about it. I'm free Monday. I'll call you to arrange something."

"Perfect. Now I have to get going and be home for Paige."

The clan brought their dishes to the sink and offered to help clean up.

"No," I protested. "You guys get on home. I don't mind doing it, and it'll help me clear my mind as I work on figuring out a plan."

After everyone left, I thought how proud Butch would be of them. But maybe he would be shaking his head at me.

Chapter Twenty-Two

Michigan City

Anne picked me up at ten on Monday morning, and we headed south on I-96. That late February day was clear, cloudless, and an unseasonably warm forty degrees. Over the few previous days, I had Googled and printed information about Michigan City to share with Anne during our drive. We had both driven past the Indiana exit off I-94 during our trips to Chicago and back but never had a reason to stop—not even at the Lighthouse Outlet Mall.

I informed Anne that Michigan City had originated around 1860. A grainy black-and-white photo from the late 1800s showed a Smith Brothers cough drops factory and also a Pullman-Standard railcar plant. The town used to be composed of 70 percent full-time residents and 30 percent summer ones. Today, the ratio is reversed. Many of the original eclectic cottages along the lakefront were torn down and have been replaced with very luxurious homes used only in the summer and on fall weekends.

So, it looks like this Elaine Peters lives on Lakeshore Drive in the Long Beach subdivision...wherever that is."

"We'll find it. The town is really small. But first, let's have lunch."

We drove slowly along Franklin Street, which wasn't a problem, as there was no traffic at all. Only a few cars occupied the angled spots all along this sleepy main street.

"Pull in here, honey, right in front of the *Michigan City Dispatch* office. Wonder how long small local papers will survive. Oh, it looks like there's a lunch spot down the block."

We strolled by an aptly named shop—the Bookstore—and walked into the Cozy Kitchen. Not much originality, at least on this street. A bell over the door tinkled as we entered. Seven heads at the counter turned in unison, nodded at us, and turned back to their lunches—just like in an episode of *Gunsmoke*, except this wasn't a saloon. We sat at a table covered in a green-and-white-striped tablecloth. Menus slipped into plastic sleeves were already on the table, propped up by the napkin holder and mustard and ketchup bottles. *Any small town, USA*, I thought. Comforting.

The menu, with its standard fare of chili, hamburgers, hot dogs, grilled cheese, and fries had been brought into the twenty-first century with offerings of pita sandwiches, flatbreads, and salads with arugula and goat cheese. Anne eyed the revolving circular display of homemade pies at the end of the counter but decided on just a bowl of chicken noodle soup. For me, a BLT seemed to fit the atmosphere.

Our waitress had a friendly, freckled face framed with strawberry-blond curls down to her shoulders. She took our order and whipped around to deliver it to the kitchen. When she returned with our coffee, I said, "We're visiting town to look for an old acquaintance of mine, Elaine Peters. Do you know her?"

"Anyone who's lived here for a long time knows her. That's for sure. She's a real sweetheart," the waitress said. "Elaine manages the Jolie Hair Salon on Seventh Street. Turn left out of here, walk two blocks, and turn left again, two doors down."

After she left the table, we grasped hands and grinned at each other.

"Oh my God. Are we really going to find her, Mom? After all this time, she really has been this close? Unbelievable."

"It looks like it. Oh, I don't know if I'll be able to eat my lunch! My stomach is doing flip-flops, and my heart is racing."

"Same here, let's calm down and plan our approach. First, we'll just check her out, look like we're planning to make a hair appointment. God knows I could use a trim, so it won't be a stretch. This is really fun."

"No, Anne, it's not. What if she isn't in town right now? And what will we say to the woman if we do find her? What if she's hostile? Or denies knowing anything? Or calls the police because we're harassing her? What if we find nothing out? What if we do find something? Then what? Oh man!"

"Mom, wait. First things first. Don't get ahead of yourself. And this is what you've always wanted to do: find the girl in the polka-dot dress."

Our waitress deposited our lunches in front of us and asked if there was anything else we needed. I asked if they served drinks—a Bloody Mary would be perfect. But the answer was no. The unsettled feeling remained with me, and I was only able to eat half the sandwich, which stuck in my throat. Patiently, I waited for Anne to finish the apple-crumb pie she couldn't help adding to her order. I didn't even ask for a taste.

Out on the street, we didn't have to zip our jackets, as the sun was bright overhead and there wasn't any wind. We passed a trendy-looking boutique named Just the Right Thing.

Any other time, we would have turned into it without even asking each other. Not today. Next was an Ace Hardware—hard to believe it had survived the influx of the big-box stores. The next two storefronts were empty. I peeked into the window of a small florist shop on the next block. A woman was peering over her glasses at the white calla lilies she was putting into a vase, frowning as she did so. Then she looked up at me and waved. I took this as a good sign.

We turned the corner and stopped in front of the Jolie Salon, its name written in gold script across the front window. Pink dragonflies were painted at the beginning and end of each letter. A pink eyelet valance ran across the top of the window. We stepped into the shop. The interior was an example of the nineties' "mauving of America," a term coined by a decorator friend. An elderly woman was under a dryer, her aqua brush rollers peeking out from the hood. Two of the four charcoal faux-leather chairs were occupied, one with a patron in mid-cut and one with a woman having her hair blown dry. The stylists were in black yoga pants, black long-sleeved shirts with the salon logo in gold on the sleeves, and black gym shoes. The hair dryer was switched off.

"Welcome," said the stylist, a skinny, pale girl with short, spiked black hair. Her name, Angela, was embroidered in pink on her shirt.

"How can we help you? Do you need an appointment? Claudia here will be free in about twenty minutes."

"Not today," I said. "We were looking for Elaine Peters. She's an old friend. She went to high school with my sister in West Battle Creek, Michigan. Plus, I want to check out the area for a family reunion for this July. We found out Elaine works here."

"That she does, but this is her afternoon off. She just left an hour ago. Who should I tell her was trying to find her?"

Anne quickly chimed in, "Oh, don't worry about it. We'll stop in at her house. Just thought it would be fun to see where she works and surprise her."

"Well, this is the spot. Elaine has managed this salon for years, and she's a dream to work for. Have fun catching up."

"Will do. Thanks for your help."

As we left the shop, I turned and saw Angela take her cell phone from her side pocket and start dialing. Was she calling Elaine and warning her? Or was she just calling home? Calling a boyfriend? She smiled and waved at me. It was probably an innocent call...or she was a good actress. Anne witnessed this too.

"Oh, boy, what do you think?" she asked. "Wasn't our story good enough?"

"Don't know. Let's just get back to the car and find this Long Beach."

Lakeshore Drive followed Lake Michigan going east. Right away, we noticed stop numbers on posts on the lake side of the road. Some of them indicated public access to the beach. As we drove by stop twenty-eight, we realized we had passed Elaine's address. To turn around, I pulled into a large circular drive in front of a looming white-brick home on the right side of the street.

"Boy," I said, "talk about cutting off the view from the cottages behind!"

"Really. Kind of a shame," Anne said.

Elaine's home was on a corner. We turned left to park on the gravel space alongside her house and walked to the front. The two-story Cape Cod home had charcoal cedar siding trimmed in white. The front lawn held a spreading oak tree at least a hundred years old. Snow still covered the area, but gardens were evident along the front and on angles at each corner of the lot. We looked at each other as we walked up the steps of a wide white porch with handrails. Anne rang the doorbell and banged the black wrought-iron knocker on the door, which was painted a deep red. My ears strained for any sound within. Nothing. Seconds passed. Then interminable minutes. Still nothing.

"Not home," Anne said.

"Nope." My shoulders sagged...was it disappointment or relief?

"Let's get back in the car and decide what to do. Maybe we should have asked for her phone number. The White Pages site didn't list one. She most likely just has a cell."

As we started down the steps, a woman was coming up from the beach between two houses across the street. She was tall and dressed in a black, puffy, knee-length jacket, a black-and-white hound's-tooth scarf, skinny jeans, and knee-high, trendy navy rubber boots. Her hands were in her pockets, and her head was bare and bent down as she walked. As she got to the road, she looked both ways for cars and then at us. She straightened up, smiled, and came toward us. Her hair was light brown with some golden streaks. Oh, yes. Elaine was a sixty-eight-year-old woman with a distinctive pug nose.

"Can I help you with something?" she asked, her voice friendly and soft.

"Elaine Peters?" I began.

"Yes?"

"My name is Margo Huver."

No recognition was obvious in her face. But why would it be? My interaction with Sirhan had been two years before hers.

"And this is my daughter, Anne."

Puzzled, she looked from Anne's face to mine. I was pretty sure now that Angela from the salon had not called her.

"Miss Peters...I know this seems very strange, but I would really like to talk to you about something that happened to me many years ago—something that I need to find out about as much as I can. We drove here this morning from Grand Rapids." I suddenly felt that we might be kindred spirits in a way. I knew so much about her, yet not enough. And I sensed that she too had gaps in her past or maybe unexplained memories.

"How could I possibly help you? What is this about? And how did you find me?" she asked.

"The Internet, of course, and a waitress in town told us where you worked. You deserve an explanation for me being here. But it's long and involved and—"

Elaine cut me off. "OK...I admit I should be frightened, but I'm not. Those in town who know me would have never have given you any information if they thought you two were dangerous. But it's cold out here; come on in. I have some time before a friend picks me up for a meeting at Notre Dame, my church, and then we're joining friends for dinner."

"Wonderful," I said as Anne and I followed her up the steps. She simply twisted the tarnished doorknob, and we were led in.

"You don't lock your door?" Anne couldn't help asking.

"Nope. Not during the day. I wasn't gone long. Lake Michigan in the winter isn't usually as appealing as it was today."

The front porch had roll-out windows on three sides and natural wicker furniture upholstered in fabric the same shade of red as the front door. Elaine slipped off her boots in the front room, which was parlor-like, with mixed styles of upholstered furniture in earth tones. Distressed oak tables sat among antique over-stuffed chairs and two traditional love seats. On the mantel, a watercolor painting of a lighthouse leaned against the wall.

"Is that the lighthouse at the end of Mission Peninsula in Traverse City?" I asked her.

"Yes. I bought it at the ArtPrize festival in Grand Rapids a few years ago. I went to college in Grand Rapids for a year and feel compelled to go back now and then. Here, give me your coats and have a seat." She tossed them over the banister with her own and continued. "Let me get you something to drink. Coffee? Tea? Soda?"

I couldn't trust myself to hold a cup without shaking. "Water would be great."

"Me too," Anne said as she gently tapped her fingers on her knee—always a sign that she was anxious about something.

"OK. I'll reheat myself some coffee. I'll just be a minute."

I looked around her home some more. The dining-room furniture was a maple-colored mission style, and the bronze chandelier finished off the simple yet inviting room. Through an archway was the kitchen, bright yellow with white cupboards and lots of sunlight. Elaine returned with our water and went back for her coffee. Anne and I sat on a love seat and dared not talk. Our exchanged looks conveyed our thoughts. How to broach the subject?

I needn't have worried. Elaine set her mug on an end table and was swallowed up in an overstuffed chair covered in a wheat-colored fabric with pale-green palm fronds.

"So, what is this long and involved story of yours, and what does it have to do with me? I have to admit I'm nervous."

"Of course, you are," I said. "Here we are, strangers. But thank you so much for being so gracious."

She slowly nodded. The time was now to begin the saga. I set my water on a square glass coaster on the coffee table.

"In 1966 in Grand Rapids, a peeping-tom type stalked me for about six months, first looking in my window, then lurking in the yard, rattling windows and doors, skulking around the neighborhood. I had four small children under five, and my husband worked nights. Being scared to death all the time was awful. Then, in 1968, I saw his face on television." I paused. "My stalker was Sirhan Sirhan."

She reacted like everyone else who heard my story for the first time.

"What? RFK's assassin? Are you sure?"

"Yes, I'm sure. The first time he was at our home, I was face-to-face with him for several seconds. Trust me. It was him."

"Wow. Wow. Didn't you to go the police?"

"Yes. And believe me, they were no help. Maybe they couldn't have helped. I don't know anymore."

She grabbed her mug and held it with both hands, not drinking. "I worked on Robert Kennedy's campaign for a while—dropped out of college to do so. And then, and then, and then—I don't know. I just don't know." Her head then hung down toward her mug.

Chapter Twenty-Three

Woman in the Polka-Dot Dress

I became rigid, frozen in the chair. Elaine was so still and hardly seemed to be breathing. Then she slowly lifted her head and looked at us, absently, forlornly.

Anne finally spoke, "Elaine, it's all right. We're only here to find some answers for my mother, who finally has the courage to seek them out. Could you please tell us about your life, beginning with White Rapids College?

"I've never spoken about that time except to a psychiatrist."

"You saw a psychiatrist?" I asked. "Did that help you at all?"

"No. I could never fill in some of the blanks from my past. She even hypnotized me—more than once. And...nothing."

Sirhan had been hypnotized in prison willingly, several times, to try to get him to recall why he had been in the Ambassador Hotel and why he'd shot Robert Kennedy. Nothing surfaced. Elaine's and Sirhan's experiences were parallel. I knew I had to contain my excitement or any reaction so she would continue. This was very difficult. I finally had the threaded needle in my hand and could not risk dropping it.

"Elaine," I said, "you could help me fill in some of the blanks from my past. Would you? Please?"

"I just don't understand what my life has to do with yours." She took a breath. "But if my story helps, then I will tell it. But first, I need more coffee. I'll bring a pitcher to refill your glasses." She left the room, and once again, Anne and I exchanged glances—hopeful and excited ones this time. Elaine returned with a pale-green water pitcher in almost the same pattern as my mother's Depression glass collection and refilled our glasses. She carefully put the pitcher down on a *Time* magazine that was on the coffee table. I flashed back to the 1968 *Time* with Bobby on the cover. Elaine retrieved more coffee and then sat down with us.

"Listen," she said. She took a sip, paused, and sipped again. Holding the mug with both hands on her lap, she continued. "You experienced this stalking in Grand Rapids in 1966. I was still in high school in Battle Creek. I just don't know what you're getting at."

"Elaine," I gently said, "I am not exactly sure either yet. But I know you and I are connected, though we have never met before today. And I know we both have parts of our pasts that need to be figured out." I leaned toward her, looking right into her wary eyes.

"Please tell us about your experiences at White Rapids."

She pursed her lips, lifted her chin, and peered up at the ceiling. Anne and I stared at her, and I struggled to remain composed. This was it—the culmination of months of following my obsession, either to stitch everything together or to be left with just an unfinished and useless remnant. Regardless, I had to know what I would hold, once and for all.

Elaine sat up straighter and squared her shoulders.

"OK. This was a long time ago, but I think everyone remembers the beginning part of any experience. I was excited to go to White Rapids College. The college was new and seemed welcoming. The smallness of the campus and number of students appealed to me. I had visited Michigan State, and although the university was beautiful, I was overwhelmed by its size. White Rapids College was a much better fit. Also, it wasn't far from home. Some of my classmates headed way east or west, but not me. I liked the idea that I could go home as often as I wanted. Turned out, I loved college life and didn't really go home that much."

"Me too," said Anne. "I went to Michigan State, and after a little bout with homesickness, I realized my life was there—not just for the parties and fun dorm living but for some of the truly amazing courses and professors too. I loved that part."

Good going, Anne, I thought. *Push Elaine toward what we need to hear.*

"I know. I was a shy and introverted young girl and not yet sure of what to study. My counselor helped set up my classes, mostly just covering requirements needed for graduation. One of those classes was wonderful." Elaine looked away and then back at us with a small smile.

"It was Intro to Political Science. This class opened a whole new world to me. Our country was in turmoil on so many levels, but the times were exciting too. To say nothing of the fact that we girls were finally allowed to wear slacks—that's what we called pants then—to class. Hard to believe, isn't it? My grandnieces roll out of bed in their pajamas, plop on a baseball cap, and they're off to class. The alpha and omega, that's for sure."

"Right," I said. Refocusing on what I needed to know, I steered the conversation back on topic. "Did you stay with a political science major?"

"Yes. The professor was able to make sense out of what was going on and to apply the principles we learned to actual current events. I was enthralled with the class."

Anne asked, "What about the professor? I know some of mine made a difference in some of my choices for future classes." That was my girl again, her sweet face masking her motives.

"Well." Elaine raised her eyebrows and smiled slyly. "I did have a mad crush on my Intro prof. Do you really want to hear this?"

I wanted to scream, *"Are you kidding?"* But I just nodded, smiled, and said, "Sure."

"Well, he was in his early forties. Tall. Thick black hair that was a bit wavy and kinda curled a little in the back. He wore the academic uniform of the time: khakis, brown suede hush puppy oxfords, powder-blue shirt—no tie, of course—and a brown or navy corduroy blazer with suede patches on the elbows. But his eyes, oh my—a piercing cobalt blue. And that was before tinted contacts, so they were the real deal. His gaze would draw your eyes directly to his, almost like a magnet. A real hottie, as my neighbor's girls say these days. So, needless to say, I took two of his poli-sci classes the next semester: Political Theories and also Politics and the American Government. I made sure to check the professor's name after the course description... yep...his name was Dr. Leonard A. Burgman."

I wanted to jump up and down, grab her by the shoulders, shake her, and yell, "What else?" But I didn't. Instead, I just took a long drink of my water, and I did not look at Anne.

"Are you sure this is important?" Elaine tucked her chin-length hair behind her ears. "I mean, what do you need to know?"

"I'm not exactly sure," I lied. "I'm just interested in your life at White Rapids to see if anything connects with me or my life. Please go on. Anything more about this Professor Burgman?"

"Um. Well, of course, all the girls in his class were in love with him, some obviously flirting with him in class, on campus, and probably also in his office. I was too shy for that. I rarely spoke up in class because I didn't want to stumble over my words or not seem intelligent enough. He didn't wear a wedding ring, so I admit I daydreamed about him. Even the boys in the class seemed drawn in by his charisma, and they paid attention to every word. I can't believe I'm remembering all this stuff. Haven't thought about it in years. I guess once I stopped worrying about the months I couldn't remember, that whole time was put away for me. So I'll finish with this part of my life.

"I sat in the back of his classes. But about the middle of the second semester, this dreamboat seemed to be looking at me more and more. He gently drew me into class discussions, boosting my confidence. I was so flattered. I figured he did this with all his reluctant students. But eventually, I discovered that he did not. For once in my life, I seemed to be a teacher's favorite. One day as I was leaving class, Professor Burgman stopped me and asked me to stay after for a minute. Once we were alone in the room, he put his hand on my shoulder and said, 'I was telling my wife about you—about how you've been improving in my classes each week and seem to be less introverted, since you add a lot to class discussions now. She said that you could probably use a home-cooked meal and some time off campus for a change. So we wondered if you could come for dinner Thursday? Class is over at five, and you could ride home with me after class. Or do you have a car?'

"I tried not to appear flustered. A wife? Of course, a man like him would be married. Go to his house? In his car? I just nodded at first and then choked out the words that I would be delighted to come. Yes, I said the word *delighted.* My roommate at the time, Linda, was very different from me. She was from Grosse Pointe Shores, a ritzy suburb of Detroit, and her dad was an executive at Ford. Her clothes were all Villager outfits, and she had eight pairs of different-colored Capezio ballet flats. Remember those?"

I simply nodded that I did, even though I wanted to jump out of my seat. I didn't care about the roommate's wardrobe at all. I wanted to know what happened at the professor's house.

Elaine continued. "She partied a lot and had a big circle of friends, but she did get her studying done. And we got along great. When I told her about my invitation, at first she admitted she was pretty jealous, as any of his female students would be. But then she asked if anyone else was going. I told her I didn't think so. She thought the whole thing was a little weird. But I assured her it wasn't. His wife was making the meal, and she would be there.

"On Thursday I borrowed Linda's deep-pink cable-knit crewneck sweater and deep-pink, plaid A-line skirt. I had to settle for my own cheap black flats, though. It's funny how I remember exact outfits I wore on various occasions. Anyway, after class, there I was in the front seat of his dark-green Oldsmobile 88. I shouldn't have been nervous because the conversation was really easy. We pulled into a blacktop driveway next to a two-story white-brick home with black shutters and shiny black double doors.

"The house was a little bit bigger than those in the rest of the neighborhood—kinda nice for a college professor back then. His wife was very pretty and friendly, but definitely a Donna Reed type, complete with a navy shirtwaist, pearls, and white cardigan. Anne, you've probably never heard of Donna Reed, have you?"

"Not really," Anne answered.

I filled her in. "She was in a sitcom in the fifties and sixties, and she was always perfectly dressed like that with her blond hair in a flip. She was the ideal housewife at the time and totally unrealistic."

"I get it," Anne said. "So this Mrs. Burgman? What else about her?"

"She was very sweet. Smiled cheerfully at me and adoringly at her husband. I was prepared to hate the woman, but there was nothing about her to hate. I was surprised at how dull she seemed, though. To me, her husband was so smart and engaging, and she paled beside him. That was my take that night, anyway. I can't remember what food was served; I was so in awe of just being there. And they both made me feel very special. The evening was wonderful."

"What time of year was that? And did you ever go back there again?" I asked.

"It was the beginning of February. And yes, I had dinner there once a week without fail until the end of April. By that time, I felt like one of the family. Looking back, I wonder how Mrs. Burgman felt about that...making dinner for me and all. But then, nothing about her demeanor ever varied. She either really enjoyed my company or was just pleasing her husband."

"What about the other students or your roommate? What did they think? I could imagine emerging jealousy or suspicion or something."

"The Burgmans asked me not to let the other students in class know, for that very reason. I was only too happy to comply. The whole thing was delicious for me...being singled out, pampered, having great discussions with Dr. Burgman. Mrs. Burgman became less and less part of the evenings, just serving the meal and cleaning up and quietly working on her needlepoint. Boy, I can picture her in a brown chintz chair, squinting under a floor lamp, the needle going up and down. Brother! I haven't thought about this in years, yet it is all so vivid. Am I boring you?"

"Oh no!" We exclaimed in unison. (Later in the car, Anne said she had yelled in her head, "No freakin' way!")

Elaine continued "My roommate grew more uneasy about the situation as time went on. She didn't like the fact that he would pick me up in different spots on the campus or in the city. She kept saying, 'icky, icky, icky' and asking me if he ever came on to me or flirted or hugged me. I told her that nothing like that ever happened, that our relationship was very intellectual, and that I never let on that I had a crush on him. She scoffed at that and let me know that he wasn't stupid and said for me to be careful. She also thought I was too consumed with the Burgmans and my classes. She would drag me to parties on the weekends. To me, the college boys were so immature, and the kids' only goal seemed to be just getting drunk or high. I never even went near the corner where the pot smoke was for fear it would affect me. I guess I was a nerd. But I was a happy nerd who didn't want to fit into the scene."

"I understand," Anne said. "So, did you keep taking his classes every year?"

"No. No. My life took an abrupt turn."

Chapter Twenty-Four

Elaine and RFK

Elaine paused and glanced outside for a few seconds.

"The sun is out right now, and there's no wind. Do you mind if we take a walk on the beach for this part of the story? I have scarves and gloves and spare boots I keep for my nieces or book-club ladies."

This hadn't been part of the plan, but I was not about to rock the boat at this point.

"Sounds great. Anne?"

"Of course. And I have boots and stuff in the trunk. Always kept them handy for our drives from Chicago to Grand Rapids and back all those times. I'll go get them and meet you outside." Anne grabbed her coat and went out.

I followed Elaine to her back hallway. Lined up under a shelf with scarves, hats, and gloves in wicker bins was a gray Rubbermaid mat holding three assorted pairs of boots. Elaine handed me some neon-green Duck Boots...circa 1976.

"These should fit, Margo. And here's a hot-pink hat and a yellow scarf. Everyone will see you coming!"

We laughed, and I easily slipped into the boots.

"Not sure I'll need the hat, but I'll bring it," I said.

Once ready for our walk, we joined Anne out front. She raised her eyebrows at my outfit.

Elaine said, "When no one is home across the street, I use their stairs down to the beach. Otherwise, the public access is down a bit, at stop eighteen." She led the way.

I have to admit I had never walked a beach on Lake Michigan in the winter. What a wonderful exception this day was. Huge, crystal ice chunks still lined the sand, to eventually melt and add to the water table. The air was so clear that the Chicago skyline, slightly to the northwest, was visible in light gray. Small, smooth, navy-blue waves rippled toward shore, not a whitecap to be seen. We all stopped to gaze at this magnificent Great Lake. I couldn't see the Pentwater shore to the northeast, the home of our campsites, but I could surely picture it. We began to walk east, and Elaine steered us back to 1967.

"So...the last part of second semester, Dr. Burgman focused all of our discussions on Robert Kennedy and his quest for the presidency. Honestly, I was so enamored with Dr. Burgman, I would have bought into his support for Bozo the Clown. But the more Dr. Burgman spoke, and the more I learned about Senator Kennedy, the more earnest I became in my admiration. Why wouldn't Bobby appeal to young people? Right, Margo? Our country was really a wounded nation. We had lost our beloved president...and to violence, no less. The Vietnam War was in our living rooms as we witnessed mangled soldiers on stretchers and fire consuming thatched huts as villagers ran for their lives. Inner cities had experienced devastating riots. I remember my aunt saying that our problems were now moral ones, and we were no longer the admirable pillars of the free world. Of course, in retrospect, our previous history hadn't been all that stellar, but the perception of us was. And with all the information we have today about everything everywhere, I don't think any glossy veneer is ever possible again. A good thing, I guess."

Listening to Elaine brought those times right back in front of my face. True, I had been very busy raising our family and working in our business; I'd barely had time to read the paper. But I always listened to the radio and watched the news. And I too had been enamored with Bobby Kennedy.

Elaine was now talking about the professor again.

"What Dr. Burgman stressed that fired up my idealistic self was Kennedy's focus on fighting poverty. Here was this ultra-privileged man who really seemed to understand the poor and how poverty was holding our country back. I heard him more than once refer to poverty as 'the disgrace of the other America.' So, there I was with stars in my eyes for two older men.

"I don't remember when exactly, but Dr. Burgman's suggestions gradually convinced me to take a break from college and work on Kennedy's campaign. White Rapids would always be there, he said, but the opportunity to be part of the political science I was studying wouldn't be. I'm not sure of the logic of that now, as I did not return to college in the end. But then, I was hooked. And I also see now that he was prepared to answer any question or insecurity I had.

"Where would I live when I couldn't stay in the dorm? Well, there was a big, old, faded yellow frame house in the hill section very near downtown, that held a campaign headquarters, and some of the workers lived there. The headquarters was on the main floor in the living room and dining room. Money, too, seemed like a huge hurdle, but the campaign committee had some discretionary funds, and I also pursued a part-time job at Herpolsheimer's. I felt inexperienced and new to all this campaigning, but I was assured that the staff would determine how I could contribute. I would get to do more than stuff envelopes because of my connection to Dr. Burgman. Any doubts I raised were countered in detail. The man had done his homework. That was obvious."

Anne then asked, "What about your parents? No way would all that have flown with mine."

"To make a long story short, my aunt worked on the RFK campaign in Detroit, and she convinced my parents that it would be a chance of a lifetime, and so on and so on, and it was settled. Sooooo...I started as a gofer, but I didn't mind. This was exciting, heady stuff. Everyone was young and energetic and focused. The division of labor really worked, and we were in close quarters, so ideas and creativity flowed throughout the place. I loved it. Eventually, I learned the ropes of the whole operation."

"Was Dr. Burgman involved with any of this? Did you still see him?" I asked.

"He didn't do the day-to-day stuff. About once a week, he traveled around the state and gave speeches—wonderful, stirring speeches. And, yes, I still had dinner at his home often."

On our walk, we were just about to turn back. I had to get what I needed to know while Elaine recalled those times years ago. I stopped and turned to her.

"Elaine, do you remember anything odd or strange about those days? Any little detail? Anything at all?"

"Why would you ask that?" She folded her arms and grabbed her elbows. "How would you know about anything strange?"

I gently answered, "Because strange, weird things happened to me too. I promise I will make everything clear soon. Please just tell us."

We walked silently for about a hundred yards. I fought to keep my pace as slow as hers. I fought not to beg her to continue. I hoped Anne could do the same.

Finally, her voice shaky, Elaine responded,

"Again, I haven't talked about this for years, not since the psychiatrist sessions. But here goes. Please don't think I'm crazy. But then again, you want to know. Back then, I had a pale-green jewelry box. The top was tufted with little seed pearls. Once when I opened it, I found a necklace and matching earrings. They were not my style at all, and the price tags were still on them. Pretty expensive too. I asked around the house, but no one claimed them. And once, a lilac fur-blend sweater appeared in my closet. This time, no price tags. I asked the others, and they were as confused as I was. I think some of them started thinking I was odd, so I never brought up anything like that again."

"Did you tell Dr. Burgman about all this?" I asked.

"No. I didn't want him thinking I was crazy. But then, one time I was over for dinner, and I noticed a beautiful cut-glass vase on the buffet in the dining room. I asked Mrs. Burgman if it was new. She cocked her head to one side and told me I had given it to them weeks before to thank them for all the dinners. Didn't I remember? I did not. Not at all. And how could I have afforded such a gift? I covered by saying I had had trouble choosing between two and forgot which one I'd chosen. The Burgmans both seemed to accept this explanation, but they must have thought something was the matter with me. A few other smaller things turned up in my room. I figured that someone was messing with me, but I couldn't imagine why. I never questioned anybody about any of it."

She turned left, her hands now shoved into her pockets. "Here are the stairs we want. Let's go back in."

As we followed Elaine up, what she had told us spun around in my head. Once the spinning stopped, the incidents flew to separate spots in my mind. OK. Elaine had been spending more time with the professor, and at the same time, unexplainable objects were turning up in her house or his. Dr. Burgman had been the professor involved a few years before in the MKUltra project. Could he have been practicing the technique on Elaine? To get her to shoplift? And then to do more? And to have no memory of what happened? Two years before, could he have preyed on the loner Sirhan, preparing him for the assassination? What about the professor's wife? If Elaine was being psycho-programmed, where was Grace?

We settled back in Elaine's living room, and this time she brought out some brie and crackers and green grapes. And we all decided on coffee. I asked, "All the times you were at the Burgmans' home, was Mrs. Burgman always there?"

"Most of the time she was. But often after she cleaned up the dishes, she would go to her professor's wives' club, some kind of do-gooder group. Why? What does she have to do with anything?"

"I'm not sure. I'm just curious about their relationship. Did you notice anything questionable or different about them?"

Elaine bit her upper lip and seemed to search her memory. "No, they were pretty typical, I guess. The one out-of-the-ordinary incident was when he surprised her by suggesting they bring the washer and dryer up into their big mudroom at the back of the house—to make that chore easier, he said. And he told her she wouldn't have to go down to that creepy basement again. After she got over her surprise, she was happy about it. And that was what they did.

"Excuse me a minute. I'm going to call my friend and tell her I'll meet her at church later."

Anne reached for a cracker and strained her neck to make sure Elaine was out of earshot.

"Holy crap, Mom. The wife no longer going in the basement. Odd stuff happening to Elaine. This is it. This is it. What are you going to tell her? That she may be a murderer? She's such a neat lady. What are you going to do?"

"I don't know. I don't know. There's more to find out first. Just stay cool."

When Elaine returned, I was sipping my coffee. She didn't sit down, and her eyes bore into mine.

"So. Am I getting closer to what you're looking for? I just don't get any of it, and I'm beginning to think all this is unfair."

I nodded. "I know, Elaine, but trust me, we're getting very close to tying our stories together. I mean it. Please, just a few more questions to fill in some holes, and we will leave you."

Anne added, "And we can't tell you how much we appreciate your hospitality and helping us strangers—really."

Elaine slowly sat down and smiled a little. "I can't believe you're here in my home, on my beach, in my past. No one would believe that I'm allowing this, I am sure. But, Margo, you are very compelling, and something told me to trust you. I don't know. This whole thing is crazy." She sighed. "OK, what's next?"

Chapter Twenty-Five

Elaine and the Campaign

I knew we had come pretty close to losing Elaine, and I couldn't blame her. And I knew I had to decide when to tell her about Sirhan and me. The timing would be important and delicate. I didn't want to offend her or confuse her more—or worse, scare her. My instincts needed to be sharp to handle this correctly. So I smiled and moved her along in her story.

"I can't imagine how wonderful it must have been to be part of Bobby's campaign. I remember the scads of young people really mobilizing behind him. I was too busy with my kids and husband to get involved, but I so admired those who did. I felt that this was our generation's candidate and hope."

Elaine's eyes lit up, and she sat up straight. "Oh yes. We all worked very hard, but it was worth it because we were so energized by this man. Like I said, I began as a gofer but ended up doing mailings, calling potential donors, scheduling campaign stops throughout Michigan with the various head-quarters, and sending out canvassing teams—you name it. I eventually traveled all the way to Mackinaw City to help organize their efforts. All by myself, I might add. Dr. Burgman rented a car for me. And he was the one instrumental in getting me my next assignment." She took a sip of her lukewarm coffee, and as before, I purposely did not even glance at Anne.

Elaine continued. "Los Angeles, California. I couldn't believe it. California! My first plane ride! And I was to work in the central headquarters there. The Democratic Party's nomination pretty much rested on California. This was huge. I couldn't wait to tell my parents. Their simple little girl from Battle Creek was going big-time."

"When exactly was this?" I asked her.

"I had to be there ready to work by May 18. We had about a week and a half for the final push."

Anne asked, "How did you know what to do when you got there? I would have been pretty intimidated."

"Oh. Dr. Burgman and my supervisor prepped me for everything. Once on the plane, I couldn't believe the confidence people had in me. I was met at the gate. Remember back in the day, when anyone could be at the gate? A young Hispanic man met me. I can't remember his name for the life of me. He was pleasant but a little brooding. On the way to the hotel, he explained the ropes—that there would always be a car to pick me up, and I was to be ready to be a troubleshooter. I never really saw him at the headquarters though. And me being a troubleshooter was accurate. I was always running around for people or having two or three of them on hold while I tried to find some information. But I felt pretty important and grown up, working in a different city and all."

I asked, "Did you ever get to meet Bobby? That would have been the best for me."

A cliché came to life as I watched her. The color drained from her face, literally from her forehead to her neck. She seemed to shrink in her oversized chair, and she gasped for air. What was I doing to her? I wanted to put my arms around her, to cradle her, to comfort her. But I couldn't. This was what I was here for. Had I gone too far? What would my selfish desire to learn the truth do to her?

Before I could react to my thoughts, Elaine leaped up and began pacing and wringing her hands. Then she stopped, looked past us, and spoke. "Eventually, I was slated to go to the Ambassador Hotel on the day of the California primary. Bobby felt that if he won there and in the rural South, he could go all the way. Poll predictions had him with an edge over Senator McCarthy. I could hardly keep my excitement in check as I waited for the car that was to take me to the hotel. Soon it showed up, with the Hispanic man driving. There was someone in the back seat, someone small. Can't remember if it was a man or woman."

My eyes widened. "And?"

She turned to me with an anguished look. "And—nothing. Nothing." She dropped her head and whispered, "I don't remember anything after that—until I woke up the next day in my hotel room. I turned on the television and learned that Bobby had been shot."

Silence hung in the room. Elaine was exhausted, and I was trying to digest what she had told us. Anne had tears in her eyes. Elaine collapsed onto her knees, this time calling out, "Why can't I remember? Why can't I remember?"

Anne helped her back to her chair. I didn't know what to do or say, if anything. Finally, Anne said, "Don't worry. Don't worry. Just tell us what you do remember. We're getting closer to the truth, I think."

"Truth? What truth?" Elaine was yelling now.

I gave her a few moments before answering.

"My truth." I paused and gathered strength. "In 1966, I was stalked for several months by Sirhan Sirhan, Bobby's killer. I've been searching for some connection between Sirhan and Grand Rapids. I found your name in an article from the *Grand Rapids Chronicle.*" I didn't want to bring up the Dr. Burgman piece yet.

"I just don't get it. I don't understand," she said.

"I don't totally yet, either. I need to hear the rest from you, and then maybe I will."

"Is there a chance my blanks will be filled in for me?" she pleaded.

"Maybe. I don't know," I answered her. *Lord*, I thought. *Am I going to destroy this woman?* The thread was becoming tightly woven around her. She could have been a patsy, the person programmed to be the trigger for Sirhan to fire shots at Kennedy and take the focus from the real killer—whoever fired the two shots from close behind the senator.

Before I could think or panic any further, Elaine drew some inner strength and said, "When I finally became aware of what happened to Bobby, I was shocked. So sick, so heartbroken. I called Dr. Burgman right away."

"Not your parents?" I asked.

"No. Probably because he had made all my arrangements, I guess. He managed to calm me down, told me he would get me a flight back to Grand Rapids. A campaign worker would pick me up and take me to the airport. And a sweet woman did just that. We sobbed all the way to the airport. The place was so quiet. People were moving trance-like, especially me. I don't know how I got on that plane."

"Didn't your parents want you to get home?" Anne asked.

"Yes. But I was pulled somehow back to campus and Dr. Burgman. He was wonderful. I stayed there for three or four days, mostly sleeping. He didn't want me watching television because I was so traumatized. Mrs. Burgman felt I should watch, but she was overruled."

"Did you read the papers about the events—the funeral, the train ride, the burial?" I asked. Could she really have known none of the details surrounding Senator Kennedy's death?

"No. I was destroyed; the life had been sucked out of me. I eventually went home. My whole future had been changed."

Chapter Twenty-Six

Then and Now

"At the time, I thought my life was over," Elaine said. "My purpose, what had consumed my every waking moment, was gone. I felt empty at the loss of Bobby and at the state of our country. When I did see Sirhan on the news, I was filled with hatred and a strange, unidentifiable feeling. And making it all worse was once I was home, Dr. Burgman didn't take my phone calls. I wrote him several times—never an answer. I just couldn't understand it. I didn't have the courage to go see him. I was devastated. A huge hole remained where he had been. I never spoke to him again. Can you believe that?"

I shook my head, but of course, I did believe it.

She went on. "I wasn't interested in college anymore. I really wasn't interested in anything. And I had trouble sleeping. My parents didn't know what to make of me. They insisted I go to our family doctor for a physical. He had been my doctor since I was born, and he sensed right away that something wasn't right with me. After ruling out anything physical, he recommended I see a psychiatrist. I was flat emotionally then and didn't care about anything, so I made an appointment. I think I told you that those sessions with him were futile because I couldn't remember what had happened in California.

He prescribed a mood elevator and sleeping pills, but I ended up throwing them out.

"My aunt, recently widowed, had bought a house in Michigan City so she could be closer to her grandchildren in South Bend. She suggested I come live with her until I figured out what I wanted to do. I thought a temporary move might be a good idea. But, as you can see, it wasn't temporary." Elaine smiled. "I went to the local junior college and got a beautician's certificate. Soon I started working at the Jolie Salon and ended up really enjoying it. Within five years, I was the manager. When my aunt died, she left me a substantial amount of money, and I was able to buy the shop and her house from my cousin."

I asked her, "And you never got married?"

"No. I had a few steady relationships, but I was never really able to go the next step, to commit. I had a hole within me that would never be filled. But despite that, I've carved a very good life here with my business, my friends, my church, my niece's family. I've been happy." She looked at us. "Will I still be happy?"

I wasn't sure how to answer her. A few words from the only play I remembered from high school, *Macbeth,* came back to me: *I am in blood. Stepped in so far that should I wade no more, returning were as tedious as go o're.* Macbeth knew he was too deep in to stop his plan. It was too late to get out now. And that was where I was.

"You've made your own happiness so far, Elaine," I said. "There's no reason you can't continue."

I told her my Sirhan story again and asked her if she had ever crossed paths with him. She vehemently denied that she had, as I knew she would.

"I'm so sorry I haven't been able to help you."

"But you have, Elaine. You have."

"How?"

"The information about Dr. Burgman...he wasn't what you thought he was. He was involved in a government-sanctioned mind-control experiment. By the time you met him, the experiment was deemed illegal, but I believe he continued it with Sirhan and with you."

She jumped up. "What do you mean mind control? What are you talking about?"

I explained. "I mean this process, called psycho-programming, hypnotizes people and uses drugs and other means to get a person to do something and then not remember anything about it. This could have happened to you."

"No! That's crazy!" She was now pacing around the room. "I certainly would know if I was drugged!"

I stood up, too, and she stopped pacing. "But you wouldn't know if you had been drugged necessarily. Did you ever see *The Manchurian Candidate*?"

"Of course," she said. "But that was years ago. And that was a movie, all fiction!"

"But, Elaine, some of that movie was based on Nazi tactics. The fact is the MKUltra project did exist." Remaining calm and reasonable was becoming increasingly difficult for me. Elaine had moved behind Anne's chair and was leaning on the back of it. Anne was a tense statue as Elaine continued.

"This is just too crazy. I can't believe any of it."

I walked over to her and gently led her to the couch. I sat beside her and took her hands. Both of ours were trembling.

"But there are parallels between your life and Sirhan's. You don't remember where those odd things came from, and you don't remember those days just before the assassination. Sirhan doesn't remember why he shot Kennedy, only that he found himself with a gun pointed at the senator, and the senator was on the ground. Teams of psychiatrists have hypnotized him and evaluated him, and they all say he's not lying about that. Just like you aren't lying about those lost days."

"How do you know all this? Why don't other people have this theory about Sirhan?"

"It's all out there in numerous books, TV documentaries, and public records of the trial. You've sheltered yourself from anything related to the assassination, which is totally understandable. But Americans have accepted that Sirhan alone is guilty. And apparently, that's what some hoped would happen. But several facts point to there being another gunman directly behind Kennedy who delivered the fatal shots."

Elaine took her hands from mine and grabbed a pink chenille throw pillow. She hugged it against her chest.

"This is too much to take in. I have so many questions..."

"I know. But I don't know if you want the answers or if they would make a difference in your life. You were just a pawn for Burgman. Look how he deserted you back then."

"Have you spoken to Dr. Burgman?" Elaine's voice quivered.

"He's dead now. But I did visit his wife at a nursing home, and she's in stages of dementia. She did remember young people being at her house and something weird about the basement."

"Oh my God. What went on there in that basement?"

"Whatever happened, nothing was your fault. But your life was cruelly altered by that man. That much we know."

"But what about you? Why are you really here?" Elaine was close to tears.

"Like I told you, it took me so many years to finally try to figure out—why me? What was Sirhan doing tormenting me and my family all those months? I've been looking for any kind of connection. And I found it. I believe that Burgman was psycho-programming Sirhan. And Sirhan stalking me all those months was just practice—practice for something horrible. Think about it. I lived just around the block from Burgman and was alone with small children at night. He only came when my husband was at work, except one time when my husband was home, but our van was not in the driveway. Once, he tried to get in the house but couldn't. He never really tried to harm me."

"And me?" asked Elaine. "He was practicing on me, having me shoplift that stuff? Why? Oh my God! I'm too scared to know." She was rocking back and forth now, and my heart went out to her.

"Maybe he needed you to be a good front for him as a backer of Kennedy, so no one would suspect him of any involvement. And maybe he cared enough about you to make you not remember that awful day."

Anne was sitting there, looking from me to Elaine and back. Her face betrayed my fear that maybe I had gone too far. I knew that was what she was thinking, but there was no stopping this conversation. It had become a runaway train.

"We can't be sure of anything, Elaine. We'll probably never know the real truth. But I do have one more question. Did you ever have a polka-dot dress?"

"Heavens! What are you talking about?"

Chapter Twenty-Seven

No Dress?

The rest of the room evaporated for me. A shaft of light from the late afternoon sun illuminated her face, now a pale white with splotches of red. I could hear my breathing and was aware of every hair on my head, and I felt paralyzed. I had never fainted but now thought I might. I couldn't speak.

Elaine kept on. "What in the world? What does a dress have to do with anything?"

The room came back into focus, and I was able to respond.

"This is very important. Did you ever have a polka-dot dress? Please?"

"No. I don't think so."

"Elaine, remember when you said you often could recall what you wore on certain occasions? I thought if you had such a dress, you would remember it."

"Well, I don't have a polka-dot dress and never did. But what could it possibly have to do with anything?"

I rose from the couch and walked across the room to sit in a chair. I took a deep breath and looked at Anne, who nodded. I was ready for my lie.

"There was a grainy photo of a girl on the day of the assassination. She had on a white dress with small, black polka dots, and—"

Elaine interrupted me. "What are you saying? Are you accusing me of being involved? Of being connected to the murder of Bobby Kennedy? The man I loved and worked for? Are you crazy? Did the picture even look like me, for God's sake? And if it did a little bit? So what? I've never had a polka-dot dress. I'm sure of it now."

Anne got up and knelt in front of Elaine, placing her hands on the woman's knees.

"That's all we needed to know. You're not the girl in that photo. You're not her. We're sorry for all we've put you through. We're not sure of anything, really. But you've been helpful to my mother." Anne stood up.

Elaine's head hung down on her chest, and there were tears.

"How?" She looked up at me. "How, Margo? Just how have I helped?"

"You've helped plenty, Elaine. The information about Dr. Burgman, especially. I knew I would never figure everything out, but this has cleared up a lot. I'm just so sorry you had to go through everything today. Really, I am."

"Just what did you two think would happen? Huh? What did you think would happen after you entered my life and turned my past inside out? You didn't even know me! Yet you felt you had some permission to do this to me? God! It's time for you to leave. Get out of my house!" She turned to go into the kitchen and then spun around. "And don't ever contact me again. Ever."

Back in the car, we just sat there. Shaken. Sad. Overwhelmed. Even though we had found our polka-dot-dress girl and verified my suspicions about Dr. Burgman, I felt no sense of victory or satisfaction. The runaway train had crashed, and a victim had been tragically hurt. Elaine was right. What had I thought would happen? Either I would have determined she wasn't the woman I was looking for and been bitterly disappointed, or she *was* the woman, and I would hurt her on so many levels. My singular quest had taken over my life, and the fallout now had so many consequences. I felt sick.

Anne was mulling over similar thoughts and finally said, "Mom, we better get going. Let's drive for a bit and then stop for something to eat. I'm too tired to drive all the way home right now."

"Fine," I said, and I reached for the lever on the side of the seat to recline a bit. I laid my head back and closed my eyes. They were dry and sandpapery. My muscles ached, and I was exhausted and weak.

We drove in silence, and I fell into that merciful half-dozing, half-awake state.

"Here's the Benton Harbor exit," Anne said. "Wanna stop at that Big Boy?"

I agreed but wasn't even sure I could eat. As we stood at the hostess station, I realized how identical these restaurants were all over the state, and the décor had not been updated in years. Everything was so tacky. And "Q-Tip heads," as my mother always referred to older women with short, white, permed hair, populated 80 percent of the booths. Once seated, I looked at the glossy, colorful, laminated picture of all the desserts and zeroed in on the signature strawberry pie. That would be my dinner tonight. Anne ordered the Big Boy Combination, her standard since she was a kid. My coffee revived me, and my brain was now clear.

"OK," I began, "the only way to come out of our funk right now is to look at what we learned. I can't undo all I did to Elaine today. I can only go forward." I was rationalizing I knew—a great defense mechanism—and it sounded harsh. But that was how I coped.

"So, Anne—that was her dress. We know by her yearbook picture that she was the girl. The professor obviously made sure she wouldn't remember the dress. He must have gotten rid of it."

Anne put her fork down and stared at me. "Right. She stayed at the Burgman house for a few days. He could have easily taken it from her suitcase. He knew the LA police were looking for a young woman in that dress."

"Of course. I'm sure that is what happened. That has to be it." I thought back on my research. The police and FBI really hadn't pursued the dress angle. I remembered that at one point they had tried to pass off another campaign worker in a very different-colored dress as a suspect. She was also older and had a blond teased hairstyle, clearly not the person described by several witnesses. The authorities did not want to deal with anyone else associated with Sirhan. They wanted this lone man to be convicted and put away forever. Anne and I didn't chat while finishing our dinner. I was filing all I had learned in the right spots in my head again.

Our food had energized us a little, and we were soon back on I-94. Just as we exited north on I-96, Anne's cell phone rang. I leaned over to check the phone number on the car display. It was not familiar to me, but this was her phone, not mine. Anne pushed the telephone icon on the steering wheel to activate the Bluetooth and was greeted with "Anne? This is Elaine."

I whipped my head around and looked at Anne, and then I spoke.

"Elaine! How did you get this number?"

"Your daughter left a bright-yellow Post-it note on my counter with both your numbers. Thank you! That's how."

I raised my eyebrows at Anne, but she just shrugged.

Elaine shouted, "Well, I said I would never speak to you again. But I have to say something! I Googled the polka-dot dress information. Oh my God. She went into the hotel with Sirhan and was there for the whole shooting—came out screaming, 'We've killed him!' And you thought that was me? I was disgusted and furious with you two. I felt nauseous and threw up." She began speaking faster.

"Then I started to panic. I called my old roommate. We continue to exchange Christmas cards, but we haven't spoken for three or four years. I didn't know if I wanted her to answer or not, but she did. We chatted a bit until I came to the point. I asked her if she remembered me ever having a polka-dot dress, but she didn't. She asked why I was asking her this. I told her I was having disturbing recurring dreams, and the dress was in them. She thought awhile and told me again that she didn't remember such a dress and not to take offense, but my clothes back then were pretty basic and traditional, and a polka-dot dress would have stood out in her memory. Relieved, I thanked her and told her I would call again soon to catch up. I probably won't, as she no doubt thinks I'm crazy, thanks to you."

She seemed to gulp. Then she spoke even louder. "So that girl—that girl with Sirhan was not me, and you can be sure this *is* the last contact we will ever have." And she hung up.

Whoa. I reexamined the conversation, or rather her monologue, before speaking. She had desperately needed to convince herself that she was not the girl we thought she was. I understood that. Elaine's denial of any possible involvement rested on the college roommate's memory of a dress.

Anne interrupted my thoughts.

"Mom, Elaine is a smart woman. She could have bought that dress after leaving college, and her roommate wouldn't have known about it. She could be delusional, don't ya think?"

"No, not delusional. But she has to stay in denial, or else… or else the ramifications are too serious for her. I feel really awful for her. I do."

Anne glanced away from the steering wheel at me.

"Do you really think that's the last we'll hear from her?"

"I'm sure of it."

Chapter Twenty-Eight

June 2015

I arrived at the campsite after noon that Saturday in June. I stood on a nearby bluff, shielded my eyes, and gazed down at Lake Michigan. That day, the waves were high and a teal blue, and the midday sun glistened over the top of each wave as it sailed to shore. The beach wasn't crowded but would become so later in the afternoon when the sun was not so strong. Two large rainbow-striped umbrellas sheltered a family as they picnicked together. Three tanned, skinny teenage boys tossed a bright-orange Frisbee, one boy laughing and chasing it into the water. Walking ankle deep along the shore were three women in colorful beach cover-ups and large, floppy straw hats. These women brought to mind the time I walked that beach with Anne and Elaine in February. Different Lake Michigan shore. Different weather. Different women.

I turned away from the lake and walked on a narrow dirt path through long, swaying grass along the bluff to the cabins. Soon, everyone would arrive for a long-overdue Pentwater reunion: my sisters, Joni and Carol Ann, and their husbands; my cousins Janet, Dori, and Geraldine and their husbands; all our children and grandchildren; and my first great-grandchild, Natilee, who is a wonderful sparkle in my life. My heart hurt because I knew how Butch would have loved this. Tears clouded my vision.

Before I could be dragged down too far with sadness, my grandson, his wife, and Natilee drove up the gravel driveway in their dusty, navy-blue Honda minivan. I wiped my eyes and thanked God that my life still held so much joy for me.

By late afternoon, everyone had arrived and was unpacking and getting organized in their cabins. Most of us were way beyond tents and campers now. Some of the younger ones still camped in the state park across the street. We agreed that the grown-ups would gather after dinner for coffee and dessert. I chose the cabin Anne, Paige and I were sharing because we had the largest combined living room and dining room. The grandkids would be busy collecting kindling and retrieving logs from the pile under a blue canopy strung between two large oak trees. And they would make sure the traditional campfire would be ready by dark.

The outside of our cabin had recently been upgraded with chocolate-brown aluminum siding trimmed in a pale green. The inside remained almost as it had for forty-five years. All the walls were knotty pine paneling, and the floors were of worn, dark-oak planks. Various sizes of oval multicolored braided rugs were scattered throughout. Amazingly, the gold-speckled kitchen sink and bathroom sink, as well as the old antique brass-footed tub, remained in perfect condition. Brand-new stainless-steel kitchen appliances stood out against the rest of the furnishings.

In the living room, the two couches and four chairs were covered in blue-and-white checked slipcovers, and the end tables and coffee tables were a mishmash of types of woods and styles. Only the art-deco mahogany dining-room table and chairs were a matched set. They must have come from the owner's grandparents' home or maybe from an estate sale. A huge stone fireplace with a gray flagstone raised hearth covered almost a whole wall. The entire place was spit-shine clean, welcoming, and comfortable.

Anne had brought chili, coleslaw, and French bread for our dinner that night. Afterward, a pot of coffee brewed, and this time, another family favorite, my pineapple-upside-down cake, was ready for slicing. Paige, my sweet sixteen-year-old granddaughter, who was hurting a little less from the loss of her dad, smiled now as she headed outside to join her cousins and the rest of the family at the campfire.

The hot summer day gave way to a delightfully cool evening. Everyone wore comfy sweatshirts, jeans, and gym shoes as we gathered in our cabin around seven thirty. Michigan State, the University of Michigan, and all the directional colleges of our state were represented: Western, Eastern, Central, and even Northern from the UP. The men brought their coffee and cake to the table, and the women found spots in the living room, balancing their cake plates on their laps. The conversation at the table moved from the Tigers to the Dow to plans for a perch-fishing expedition. The women caught up on all the family news and, as indicative of some of our ages, discussed who was having what joint replaced, medications, and the strong desire to remain in our homes...always. So far, we septuagenarians were all doing pretty well.

Dori placed her cake plate on the coffee table and turned to me.

"Margo, I haven't talked to you in months. How is your research going? Find out anything new?"

Geraldine chimed in. Yes, please tell us. When I think back on how scared we all were for you—"

"And I'm still mad that we never caught that guy that night at the bar," Janet said. "If we weren't the Keystone Cops! So fill us in."

My children and sisters were pretty up-to-date already, but the rest weren't, and I wanted them to understand what my conclusions were. My threads had been stitched together now, but the fabric had frayed edges and some loose ends. That was the reality. My story was not a novel with a neatly-tied-up ending. Not all could be explained or solved.

The men tuned in to our conversation and slowly moved their chairs closer to ours. I took a deep breath and summarized, as best I could, what I knew about Sirhan, the polka-dot-dress girl, Dr. Burgman and the MKUltra Project, and from my standpoint, the botched investigation of RFK's assassination and Sirhan's poor defense at trial. I told them how I had pieced together my connection to the whole deal. That was the one thing everyone knew I was determined to figure out: my connection. Eventually, they learned what I knew of the whole story and the ramifications. All was quiet for a few moments as they mulled over what I had related. Brows were furrowed. I knew what was coming. Questions. But, probably none that I hadn't asked myself.

"Hey, guys, let's get ourselves something to drink. I would love a glass of wine. I have a twelve-pack of Miller Lite and white wine in the fridge. A bottle of red is on the counter. And then we can continue," I suggested.

One person from each cabin bolted out the door, and soon our kitchen had a fully stocked bar. We were ready for our weekend. I poured myself a healthy glass of cabernet, got comfortable in my chair, and propped my feet up on the coffee table. Two gulps of wine seemed to literally flow through my veins. Once all had a drink, the questions began.

"Oh my God, Margo. That poor Elaine! What if she thinks she *is* the one who was with Sirhan? How could she live with herself? Don't you feel bad?"

"Worse than bad," I said. "I didn't think the consequences through. Intellectually, Elaine knows that whatever happened, she isn't to blame. Emotionally? That's another story. That horrible professor—and whoever was behind him—if there was anyone—is to blame. The government sanctioning the mind-control project is to blame. I hope that knowledge is enough for her. It just has to be."

"How can you really be sure she was the one in the dress?"

"I have her description from lots of witnesses and the yearbook picture. Everyone who's seen the picture agrees with me. Right, Seamus? Anne? Todd? Dan?"

They all nodded.

"Her lost days in Los Angeles? And the unexplained stuff in her apartment?" I added.

"What do you think she'll do now?"

"I don't know and most likely never will. But I'll never stop thinking, wondering, and worrying about her. That's for sure."

"Me neither," Anne said. "We were strangers, and we crawled into her life."

"Margo, I'm just being the devil's advocate here—are you still sure it was Sirhan who stalked you way back when?"

"Absolutely. I knew it the first time I saw his face on TV. And I knew it all the other times he was on TV and in the papers. And I know it now. I really didn't have to measure the window that time to confirm that it was low enough for Sirhan, at five two or three, to look in because I knew it was him."

I totally understood that question being asked, but it always hurt a little.

"What about Sirhan Sirhan? Everyone in this country thinks he was the lone, angry assassin who is in prison for life. Remember how we felt that June day? Wow, forty-six years ago...can that be? What's your take?"

I took a deep breath and exhaled. What did I think?

"I will try to be as neutral as possible here. I think he was the loner type, had witnessed all those killings in Jerusalem, and grew up as a sad individual. His father had abandoned them, and his sister died young. I believe Professor Burgman preyed on him and persuaded him to be part of an important experiment. He might even have paid him. Sirhan, as well as other participants, had no idea what was happening to him. I think that Sirhan was programmed to stalk me so the professor could practice the mind-control technique before Sirhan was programmed to shoot Kennedy and not remember why or who put him up to it. Sirhan has always claimed that he knows he shot the senator only because people have told him, but he does not know why. He remembers standing next to a pretty girl, and the next thing he knew, Kennedy was on the ground, and he was still pointing a gun. And I told some of you that forensics said that Kennedy was killed by two shots in the neck at close range from behind. Sirhan was in front of the senator. We know that today's technology has determined from an audio tape that more bullets were fired than the eight in Sirhan's gun. And several legal experts have said that Sirhan had a very weak defense at his trial. His lawyers were concentrating on how to keep him from the death penalty and not so much on proving his innocence. So, that all said, today I feel sorry for him. I can't help it."

The questions continued.

"If all this stuff has come to light, how come he's still in prison?"

"Humph. How many officials, local or national, would be responsible if the truth came out? That he was just an accessory? That another gunman got away? That witnesses to the polka-dot-dress girl and the other young man were blown off? And on and on."

"But those people are pretty much all dead, aren't they? Wouldn't our government want the truth?"

"I used to think so, but now I don't. I was raised to have faith and trust in our government, but I don't anymore. I blew off conspiracy theories. But not anymore. I can't imagine all the untruths we have been given and swallowed in our lifetimes. Unbelievable, really."

"Where is Sirhan now? Every now and then, it's in the papers that he's been denied parole. No surprise there."

"He's been in California prisons all along and just recently was moved to another spot in Southern California. I read that several times he has been denied parole. They give him conditions. Once he was told he had to go through AA even though he hadn't had a drink for over twenty years. After that he was denied parole. He became educated at their suggestion and was still denied. He was told he didn't have any job prospects, so he couldn't be paroled. No, he will never get out of prison. That's been his life for the last four and a half decades. On September 11, he was in the shower and oblivious to what had happened to the Twin Towers. When he came out of the showers wearing a towel around him and one around his head, he was called a Muslim and put in solitary confinement though he has always been a Christian. And so the beat goes on. The injustice is monumental, as far as I'm concerned."

Anne spoke up. "Mom, we've never talked about this, but… would you ever want to visit Sirhan or give the information you have to the FBI or something now?"

"No. All this evidence I've dug up has all come out in more than one book and a documentary. I'm realistic enough to know that exposing my story wouldn't help Sirhan or anyone. It would do no good at all."

"The sixty-four-thousand-dollar question we all have, Margo, is, if your theory is true, who in the heck was behind it? Who did that Burgman guy report to? Who wanted Bobby dead?"

Ah, the biggest frayed edge. I slowly looked around the room. The eyes of all I loved were on me. How I wished I could give them a definite answer.

"For years now, and especially this last year, I've looked at this question from a million angles. Who wanted Bobby dead? Organized crime? They had the strongest motive. The KKK or other bigots? Hoffa and the teamsters? Big business? The FBI for some reason? Or perhaps someone from one of these groups gone rogue? I just don't know. I do know that Sirhan was a patsy and did not act alone. Think about it. If the police had been able to arrest him when he stalked me on Lincoln Street—and I know now how difficult it would have been then— could a few days in jail have been enough to get him out of the clutches of Dr. Burgman? Could our country's and maybe even the world's history have been changed? Could this brash, young and idealistic Kennedy brother have led us down a different and perhaps better path? I don't know. I don't know."

No more questions came forth. I felt that everyone in the room was visiting different scenarios in their imaginations. I reached for my wine glass and took a long sip. The cabin was quiet. I held my glass and looked down at the floor.

Suddenly, the screen door burst open and slammed sharply behind five-year-old Natilee.

"G.G.," she said as she jumped on my lap and luckily didn't spill my wine.

"What, sweetie?"

"Come out to the campfire now. Please?"

"Right now?"

"Yes, G.G. Come on! Come on!"

"Sweetheart, the grown-ups are talking now, and—"

Natilee put her face right up to mine and looked at me with her wide-open brown eyes.

"G.G., come out. Everybody out there already knows, but they still want you."

"Knows what?"

"Come outside and tell *me* the scary story about the face in your window. Please?"

Authors' Note

This book is historical fiction based on a true story. Everything that happened in Part I and Part II to the co-author, Margo, happened that way. Part III is fiction.

Our research and information on the RFK assassination and the theories and controversies surrounding that event came from newspaper articles from the time, public records, and several publications on the topic. The historical names are correct. Names surrounding the MKUltra Project have been changed. Other names and identifying details may have been changed to protect the privacy of individuals.

Acknowledgments

The City of Grand Rapids Archives provided a photo to be the model for the cover.

Chelsea Seekell of Chelsea Seekell Photography designed the front and back covers

The following people have been very important in the writing of this book:

Ellen Brosnahan, a published author, edited the content and posed questions for each chapter as it was written.

Cindy Nagis proofread the manuscript numerous times.

Christine Steele, a senior editor, added very valuable help for our final edit.

Jim Heintz, Angie Kowalczyk, Carol Quillin and Josh Huver made up the Grand Rapids proofreading team.

Ryan Doody, an architect, gave us the name of the architect of the Grand Rapids buildings.

Elizabeth Doody, an editor, edited the manuscript.

The following retired Grand Rapids police officers shared invaluable information on the workings of a police department in the 1960s: Jim Adams, Jerry Fein, Paul McGuire, Rich Schafsma, Bob Sucha, and Robert Wildman.

Charlie Ryan, a retired Chicago policeman, discussed the difficulty of getting an evidence tech in the Back of the Yards neighborhood in Chicago in the 1960s.

Deputy Brian Cunningham of the Naperville Police Department related how today the department takes peeping toms very seriously and has a definite protocol for protecting victims.

Paul Schrade, a close friend and advisor to Robert Kennedy, was the first victim shot along with Senator Kennedy in the Ambassador Hotel. He shared his memories of that night, as well as his quest to prove a second gunman.

Norm Dick provided hours of technical support in editing the final manuscript.

We are so thankful to our family and friends listed above for adding valuable support to our story.

About the Authors

Janet Dick spent thirty years teaching literature, creative writing, and sociology at the high school level. In addition to her own fiction, she has coauthored and published two educational instruction books. She now works with Horizons for Youth, a mentoring organization in Chicago, Illinois. Janet is working on her next book, a memoir dealing with a woman's courage against corruption. She lives in Naperville, Illinois, with her husband, Norm, and her children and grandchildren live nearby.

Margo Huver has always been an entrepreneurial and motivational force whether it is in the lives of her family members, building a business, becoming a successful Realtor, or fund raising. She is woman of many talents with a strong faith and a firm belief that anything is possible with the help of God. This strong matriarch guided her children down the path of success and conducted her business ventures with a passion for truthfulness. This is Margo's first book and she is working on a collection of short stories dedicated to her grandchildren.

73608892R00151

Made in the USA
San Bernardino, CA
07 April 2018